The Last Good Halloween

The Last Good Halloween

Giano Cromley

Tortoise Books
Chicago, IL

OCTOBER, 2013

Copyright © 2013 by Giano Cromley

ISBN-10: **0615872751**

ISBN-13: **978-0615872759**

Alkaline paper

To my parents, who taught me not to be afraid of the dark. And to my wife, who taught me how to see in it.

ELLA: Why can't you just cooperate?
EMMA: Because it's deadly. It leads to dying.

—*Sam Shepard, Curse of the Starving Class*

Chapter 1

I'm not here by choice.

Here is the middle-back seat of the Millers' Volkswagen van. It's not a slug-bug van, which would at least imply a modicum of bohemian charm. It's one of those newer Vanagons that feels like you're riding in a toilet paper tube. Plus, I can smell some kind of exhaust smell and it's making me want to hurl the beef jerky I ate at the last gas station.

A persistent southerly wind is bullying this piece of crap toward the shoulder and Mr. Miller is having a bear of a time keeping us in our lane. Mrs. Miller is focused on the road as well – brow knitted, lips pressed tight. Their son, Julian, is sacked out in the way-back seat. His body is curled in on itself, like one of those mummified children they occasionally uncover in South America. It's possible he's succumbed to the exhaust fumes, though it's more likely he's dead tired from the trials of computer camp, which is where we've been for the last week.

The Millers signed Julian up for the same computer camp as me, which happened to be in Missoula, so my mom, Debbie, worked out a deal with the Millers where she would drop us off at the beginning of the week and they would drive us home at the end.

The Last Good Halloween

Missoula is five hours away from Billings. This is the fourth time their Beach Boys mix tape has played all the way through. At this point, the harmonies are causing me actual, physical pain, like a tuning fork pressed up against my eardrum.

The Millers belong to that church on the west end of town that's shaped like a whale. Debbie took me there once or twice a couple years ago and that's how she knows them well enough to set up this ride-sharing arrangement. All in all, the Millers aren't as bad as some of the Christians you come across. But they still have their quirks, some of which I became aware of when Julian and I were test-driving a possible friendship a while back. For instance, Mrs. Miller always mutes the TV when the commercials come on. I tried telling her that the entire economic model of television is based on the sacred promise that we, the viewers, will dutifully watch the commercials, and to ignore that pact was to imperil the very medium as we knew it. She was unmoved by my argument.

Seriously, what *is* that exhaust smell? Julian's face is pale as a poltergeist, and I can't see his chest moving. I reach over the seat and poke him in the shoulder blade. His head bobs and he turns slowly to look at me. I mouth "sorry" and he reassumes his balled-up position.

So he's not dead. Just extremely tired. Which isn't a surprise. Computer camp, by definition, consists of a pretty nerdy subset of the childhood population, yet even among those myopic, asthmatic ranks, Julian stood out as a weak member of the herd. And weakness, in the lawless Thunderdome of summer camp, can attract the wrong kind of attention. Knowing this in advance, I made it my mission to keep as much distance as possible between the two of us. When Julian asked the camp director if he could switch into my dorm room, I secretly went behind his back and put the ax to that. So he spent the week rooming with some dick named Cody with a blond crew-cut. Cody and his pals took it upon themselves to make Julian's existence at computer camp sheer terror. They squirted Prell into his Crest. They turned all his pants into cutoffs. And when they couldn't come up with any other pranks, they entertained themselves by farting in his face while he slept.

"It's gotten so I can taste it in the back of my throat," he told me at lunch on Wednesday. "It's like donuts, kind of. Except not. Maybe like burnt donuts." He stuck his tongue out and scraped it with a spoon. "But I know God's putting this ordeal in front of me for a reason."

It was comments like this last one that convinced me this "ordeal" would be good for him in the long run – even if it was technically me and not God who put it in front of him. After all, we'll be sophomores at the end of the summer. If the kid doesn't toughen up, things are only going to get worse.

Of course, the same probably goes for me. Freshman year seemed to confirm my suspicions that I'm someone best defined by what I'm not: not very smart; not very good looking; not very athletic; not very popular; not a member of any identifiable social clique. Those are pretty much the only yardsticks we have to measure ourselves by. I do take consolation in the thought that I could still reinvent myself – somehow emerge from this pubescent cocoon as an all-around better person. But I pretty much *have* to think that. Because if it's not true, what's starting out as a lousy adolescence could rapidly snowball into a shitty life.

Okay, so I'm getting a headache here. That's got to be a symptom of this exhaust smell, right?

"Have you had this puppy checked out lately?" I ask toward the front seat.

"What's that, Kirby?' Mrs. Miller asks as her husband fights a particularly nasty blast of wind.

"When'd you take this rig in for service last?"

"Recently," Mrs. Miller says, turning to look at me. She's got light red hair and pale skin and is, frankly, pretty hot.

The Last Good Halloween

"Jiffy Lube?" I press, mostly because I've finally got someone's attention.

"I'm sorry?"

"Are you guys fans of Jiffy Lube? Is that where you get your work done?"

Mrs. Miller does this kind of corner-of-the-lips smile that tells me she's at least somewhat amused by our conversation.

"I took it to an independent garage near our house," she says.

"Is that where you take *your* car, Mr. Miller?"

"This is my car, Kirby," he says.

"I mean your *other* car. Your *real* car."

Though he's still focused on the highway, I catch a shadow of pride pass over his face. Mr. Miller's *other* car is a 1969 Plymouth Roadrunner, which he's had since he was in high school. He keeps it in a garage down the block from their home and supposedly only takes it out for parades and stuff. I've never seen it with my own eyes, but Julian's described it to me in great and loving detail.

"We take all our vehicles to the same guy," he says, a fine smile still lingering.

"Sure, but Jiffy Lube does a pretty thorough inspection," I say doubtfully. "I think you benefit from the peace of mind you get from a trusted national brand."

Seeing Mr. Miller puttering behind the wheel of this lame-ass minivan, when he could be strutting around in a piece of real American street muscle, makes me almost feel bad for the guy. It hints at a once-held coolness that's long since gone dormant. Which I have to think would be more painful than never being cool at all.

"Is there something on your mind, Kirby?" Mrs. Miller asks.

"Frankly, I'm concerned about your exhaust. You know, carbon monoxide's the silent killer. I don't want to sound alarmist, but Julian back here looks like he's already got one foot in the grave."

Her smile drops. Her eyes go icy. "Maybe he wouldn't be so tired if you would have roomed with him at computer camp."

Cromley

Touché. Mrs. Miller reaches forward and nudges up the volume on "Help Me Rhonda." Then she fixes her stare, along with her husband's, on the road ahead, which all of us can agree is unfolding way too slowly.

For an entire side of the Beach Boys tape, I've been pretending to be dead asleep in the hopes of letting the Millers know that computer camp wasn't a hell of a great time for me either.

Go ahead and add *Computer Whiz* to the list of things I'm not. For the past week, I spent most of my time copying other people's programming assignments and trying to load up bootleg copies of a game called "Paratroopers" onto the lab's Apple IIe's – pretty much a complete waste of Debbie's hard-earned money.

Even though my eyes are closed in feigned sleep, my internal radar is telling me we've entered Billings' city limits and we're getting close to home. I'm starting to get excited.

My stepfather, Bradley, might be back. Bradley's a CPA. Every year he works super crazy hours leading up to Tax Day. Then, to reward himself, he takes off for parts unknown on what he calls his "walkabouts." I understand how he might want, and even need, a break from Debbie and me. I don't hold that against him. But I'm constantly on edge during these extended hiati, because they always seem to last a little too long. Over the years, I've developed an informal indicator of the likelihood of his reappearance: the Bradley-Returns Index. This year it's almost July and still no Bradley. At this point, each day that ticks by, the BRI inches a little closer to zero. My hope is he'll be back when I get home and I can reset it for another year.

My gyroscopic sense tells me the wide turn the Vanagon is taking will put us smack onto Cherrybrook Drive, which means I could start yawning myself awake now and be bright-eyed by the time we pull up to the front door.

The Last Good Halloween

When I peel my eyes open, I see Julian's got his chin hooked on the seat back, peering down at me. Blond, curly hair circles his head like a wispy layer of cirrus cloud cover, his eyebrows two barely visible contrails. I have no idea how long he's been there, and the sight of him, with those dark circles under his eyes like a raccoon's mask, is enough to give anyone a start. Though I think what really spooks me is the fact that he looks like me. I don't mean in some creepy doppelganger kind of way. Just certain traits – rounded shoulders; girly hands; weak chin; wide, fearful eyes – signify that we are members of the same bottom-rung social caste.

"You look like a fetus," I whisper.

The insult seems to miss its mark because he smiles and asks, "You ready for school to start?"

"That's not for another month and a half. No one's ready, not even the teachers."

"I know. I've got church camp starting Monday." His face clouds for a moment then clears. "Do you want to come? There's probably still room."

"I guess if I had to go to church camp I'd probably be looking forward to school too."

Julian's the closest thing I have to a friend, though that's only if you accept a pretty hazy definition of that word. Yes, we spend time together socially, but that's mostly because we both know neither of us could do any better. When you're paddling around in the shallow end of the popularity pool, you can't afford to be picky.

"Almost there, Kirby," Mrs. Miller calls from the front seat. "Get your stuff together."

The Vanagon rolls to a stop in front of 343 Cherrybrook Drive, and I have an odd, unpinpointable sense that something, somewhere is amiss. I'd been hoping to see Bradley's Saab in the driveway, but the spot where he usually parks it, next to Debbie's beat up Subaru, is still empty. The BRI takes a beating it already can't afford, though there's still hope that he and Debbie are maybe running errands or something in his car.

I yank the handle on the sliding door and put all my weight into it. I step out of the exhausty interior into the hot sun. I have to visor my hand to look back into the van.

"Thank you very much for the ride," I say, with a touch of obsequiousness.

"You're very welcome, Kirby." Mrs. Miller has her window open. She's leaning out and a lock of her curly red hair is spilling over the sill. "Please give our best to your mother."

Mr. Miller angles himself over and gets into the act. "Let her know we'd love to see her at church again."

There are many responses I'd like to give, most of which would make the Millers cringe in terror and peel away in their Vanagon. Yet for some reason, I'm not feeling up to it. "I'll pass on that message," I say with a wave.

From the front door, I look back to the street and see the Millers still idling, performing the obligation of all dropping-offers to make sure the dropped-off makes it safely inside. As soon as I've got the door open, the Vanagon putters away behind me.

If I had to use a single word to describe our house I would say *modest*. One story tall with a half-finished basement downstairs. It's the perfect size for Debbie, Bradley, and me. Especially considering that for at least part of every year, when Bradley's on his walkabouts, it's just Debbie and me.

I step silently into the living room. I never announce my presence anywhere with the typical, *Hello,* or *Anyone home?* I've seen too many movies where that exact type of line can alert intruders to your presence and give them a crucial edge. So after gently closing the door behind me, I hold still and listen.

I hear nothing. And yet I detect some kind of foreign presence. After a quick inspection, though, it's clear the place is empty. I peek out the back window and catch sight of Mr. T lazing in the final warm rays of the afternoon. When I call him in, he comes reluctantly, ears tucked back, eyes shrouded behind his schnauzer-bangs, as if there are secrets he knows, but has been sworn to keep.

To round out my homecoming in style, I go to my bedroom and unstack the boxes in my closet until I get to a nondescript one wedged in the back. Inside, the object of my search: A hardcover copy of *The Art of Nude Photography*.

Last spring, in a move that was equal parts reckless and genius, I ordered it via mail from an ad I tore out of the back of a *GQ* magazine. For weeks afterwards I raced home from school in the hopes of beating Debbie to the mailbox. The one day I had to stay after school to work on a group presentation on the Trojan War, it came. That afternoon, the package – clearly opened then hastily resealed – sat on my desk. Debbie never brought it up with me and I didn't breathe a word of it to her.

As I take a position on my bed and unbutton my shorts, I begin casually flipping through the pictures. All of them are classy, with soft focus and blurry edges, which the text tells you how to recreate, since this is, ostensibly, a how-to book. After a brief perusal, I settle on one where a blond lady is stretched out in a bare room with slats of harsh sunlight falling across her skin. Her hair is swept to one side and she's got an aquamarine swath of eye shadow streaking across her eyelids. For the next five minutes, she is the sole focus of my attention.

When I'm done and cleaned up, I re-stash the book. Out in the living room, I notice on the coffee table a copy of last week's *Time* magazine. The cover is a photo of Michael Dukakis sitting on an airplane with Lloyd Bentsen. Lloyd's in the middle of saying something, and Dukakis is just grinning at him like a big-beaked gooney bird. The headline says: "The Odd Couple." Which is a sentiment I whole-heartedly agree with. But what's even odder is the fact that this magazine is here at all. Bradley has long maintained that *Time* is a front for communist propaganda and forbids the reading of it at home. That would go double for one with Dukakis on it. Its provenance here on the coffee table, in plain sight, is a mystery that bears further exploration.

I go into the kitchen and open the liquor cabinet. The trick is to find the bottle that's most nearly half full, because that's when it's hardest to notice if any's missing. I pour myself a couple fingers of Black Velvet. A little ice and a splash of orange juice to cut it and I'm back in the living room, sitting on Bradley's La-Z-Boy with the footrest levered up and the copy of *Time* on my lap. Mr. T comes in and curls up on the carpet next to me to finish his afternoon siesta. I pore over the glossy pages as if they were a foreign artifact that might provide clues to mankind's origins. Quickly, though, its newness wears off and the booze and the lack of sleep at computer camp conspire to send me into a warm and peaceful nap.

The sound of a noisy-mufflered car pulling into the driveway stirs me from my slumber. It takes a moment to remember where I am. Once I do, I decide the La-Z-Boy is as good a place as any to receive my mother and Bradley. I take a sip of my cocktail, which by now has melted and become mostly water.

The deadbolt scrapes. A shrill giggle and then the thump of something soft pressed against the door. Fumbling at the knob. The door swings open and two bodies spill into the foyer. They are holding each other in odd places, tangled, groping, their faces locked tight at the lips.

I remain seated and fully reclined. Mr. T lifts his head and perks his ears. Both of us are watching the scene in silent judgment. Slowly, one of the grapplers catches sight of me and Mr. T in the living room.

"Oh my god! Kirby." Debbie's voice is hoarse, like she just got finished yelling. "What day is it?"

The Last Good Halloween

As she unfolds herself from the other body in the foyer, it becomes obvious that it does not belong to Bradley.

"It's the last day of computer camp," I inform her.

When they're finally disentangled and standing in front of me, a wave of jerky-flavored stomach acid makes a run up my esophagus and stymies in my throat. Simultaneously, the BRI flatlines.

"Uncle Harley?" I gasp. "You?"

Harley Doherty is not my uncle, though I've called him Uncle Harley for as long as I can remember. He lives across the street from us and, up until computer camp, I was his employee – mowing his lawn once a week for fifteen bucks a pop.

"Kirby, it's good to see you," he says. He has these crazy shocks of dense brown hair that jut out from his scalp. Bristly black beard fibers flex like porcupine quills when he smiles. He looks like he might have just wandered in from the Old Testament.

"I wish I could say the feeling was mutual." I'm not sure why I say this. It's the first thing that comes to mind.

Uncle Harley looks at Debbie, then at the floor.

"Honey," Debbie tries, "I'm so glad to have you home. Are you hungry? I was about to start dinner."

I place my hands on the armrests of the La-Z-Boy. "If you didn't know I was coming home today, who exactly were you about to cook for? "

Neither of them says a word.

"Where's Bradley?" I ask cheerfully. "I wanted to pick his brain about the presidential race. See if he thinks this Dukakis guy is a real threat."

Debbie stares at me a moment, her eyes blinking a little too rapidly. "He hasn't come back from his walkabout," she says.

"I wonder what he'd say about *this*," I say, pointing to the *Time* magazine in my lap. "I can't imagine he'd be pleased."

She breathes in a long, tired breath, then lets it out and her shoulders slump. Uncle Harley's hand feels around until it finds

Cromley

Debbie's. They move into the living room and sit down side-by-side on the sofa. They're facing me now, leaning forward, forearms resting on their thighs. As a way to change up my own body language, I lift my sweating glass from the end table and take a monster gulp.

"Are you drinking alcohol?"

"It's a cocktail, Debbie. And don't try changing the subject."

Under normal circumstances, this would have elicited a sharp rebuke, but I can tell she's trying to keep things focused on the business at hand.

"Kirby," she says. "Son, we need to have a frank discussion."

"What, like a family meeting? Great, I agree. Only we can't because a certain member of our family isn't here. We don't have a quorum."

"Bradley's not your father," she says coldly.

"I'm aware of that."

"And he's not coming back."

"How do you know?"

She huffs upward and her bangs flutter lightly. "There's a lot you don't know, Kirby. About how all this works."

I'm not sure what she means by *all this*. It's just vague enough to make me think she might be speaking code for sex, which is not the terrain I'd like to have this conversation on.

Uncle Harley leans even further forward. "Listen, Kirby, I know this is going to be awkward at first, but..."

As I watch them sitting next to each other on the sofa, I realize what it was that seemed amiss when the Millers dropped me off. It wasn't anything to do with *our* house, rather it was with Uncle Harley's house across the street: a For Sale By Owner sign in his front yard. With trembling fingers I turn over the *Time* magazine. The label is addressed to him.

It's now clear I've stepped into the tail end of a chess match that's already been played without me.

"Wait a minute," I nearly shout. "Are you saying this guy's moving in? With us?"

I can tell they're both surprised at my deduction. Debbie might even be a little proud.

"As I was saying," Uncle Harley continues, "we're all going to have some adjustments to make."

"Debbie, think this through," I warn.

"It's a new situation," she says. "This can be a really good thing."

"I don't remember being asked if I wanted a new situation." As I say this, I swing my cocktail hand a little wildly, sloshing a spray of whiskey and orange juice onto the carpet.

"Kirby, honey," Debbie's almost pleading now, "everything'll be all right in no time. We just have to get used to some changes. That's all."

I set down my drink and slam the recliner lever. The footrest drops and the La-Z-Boy pops forward and I'm catapulted onto my feet in the center of the living room.

"Oh, there's going to be some changes around here!" I roar, an accusatory finger jutting deep into their personal space. "You can bet your ass on that!"

Chapter 2

The school year's starting. True to my word, there have been a lot of changes.

But in order to fully appreciate all the *recent* history, it might be helpful if I first explained some *ancient* history. Let's start fifteen years ago, with the Original Biological Contributor.

My father was a third baseman for the Billings Mustangs, our local baseball team. Debbie's never told me the details, but I've managed to scrape together a few facts. The Mustangs are Rookie-level, meaning it's the kind of team you play on for one season and then you either move up or wash out. Their courtship, therefore, was brief.

He bounced around the minors a few more seasons before either injuries or common sense told him his shot at the bigs had already passed. He never came back to Billings. When I was four, he sent a postcard. It's a picture of a nondescript baseball field with a bubbly headline that reads: "Historic Quigley Stadium, Home of the West Haven Yankees." He must have sent it just when it looked like his baseball career had stalled out, because his tone was despondent:

The Last Good Halloween

Dear Herbie [sic],
I hope your life is going alright [sic]. *Things haven't panned out for me. One thing I've learned: Never dream big, because that's how they set you up to fail. And there's plenty of buzzards waiting to fight over your bones when you do. That's all I can tell you.*
So long,
Rod (your dad)

Aside from some highly suspect DNA, that postcard was the only thing he ever gave me, and while I was too young to read it at first, Debbie saved it for when I finally could. I guess she thought it proved something, which I suppose it probably did, though I'm not sure what.

After Rod, there was a nine-year period whose most persistent domestic characteristic was instability. From ages four to five-and-a-half, she dated Nick, who was a bartender/musician. My memories of Nick are foggy. I mostly remember having to watch cartoons super quietly on Saturday mornings in order to not wake him up. For most of my seventh year, she was with Steven, a radio DJ, who always called me "little man" in his gratingly smooth radio voice. Next was Cullen, who owned a jewelry shop downtown. He was in the picture for almost two years, though I think it only lasted that long because he and Debbie actually spent so little time together. They'd maybe go on one date a month and that was it. Then there was a cop named Ray who lasted barely six months – a tenure most notable for the amount of upper-decibel arguments it spawned. There was also Frank the County Coroner, who would briefly resurface between boyfriends for a couple weeks, then disappear.

While this coterie of men varied in the amount of interest they showed in fathering me, none of them were outright assholes. They were, on the whole, decent men. The problem was that each new guy meant Debbie and I had to adopt a whole new lifestyle, foreign rituals and traditions, like some constantly re-colonized native

Cromley

people. There'd be strange relatives to meet and befriend, old high school or army buddies to have over for dinner. Debbie may have believed that each new relationship was going to be the final one, but I knew better. Eventually, either by choice or by force, they'd pick up and move on. And Debbie and I would be left wondering what parts of our lives were actually ours, and what parts were the vestigial residue from this slew of disposable men.

Then came Bradley Kellogg the CPA. Right away, it felt as if he'd been created specifically for Debbie and me. He had no real family to speak of, other than a sister he never saw, and there were no insufferable friends to put up with either. But what really set him apart was his even-keeled temperament. It didn't matter what momentary drama or despair we happened to be caught up in, he always brought to the situation a comforting rationality.

It looked like Debbie was finally ready to settle down. And Bradley seemed like the ideal person to do that with. From the moment he became the head of our household, life took on a steady, dependable rhythm. He was the stepfather equivalent of Ronald Reagan. Of course, Bradley only got a chance to hold office for five years before being impeached by the insurgent Uncle Harley. And already it feels like we're reverting to the instability of the Pre-Bradley Era.

That's pretty much it for the *ancient* history. As for the *recent* history, that basically covers the last month and a half.

It started the morning after I got back from computer camp. Specifically, it started at 5:45, with a loud thump on my bedroom window. It was the sound of the *Billings Gazette* being delivered, and the fact that it slammed into my window was not an accident. For three years our paperboy has been a kid named Jason Cipriano. He's a couple years older than me and he grew up on the next block over. I've known him all my life and always hated him. He was the kind of kid who would beg to borrow your Sunstreaker Transformer and then "accidentally" light off ladyfinger firecrackers in its tiny robot hands. As he got older, he evolved into a fairly archetypal neighborhood bully, with bad acne and food-encrusted braces, but for some reason he's always had it out for me in particular. That's the only reason I can explain for him never tossing the *Gazette* onto our front porch and instead chucking it *every morning* against my bedroom window, which is a good eight feet to the left of the porch.

This had been going on since he first started the paper route. Because Cipriano was bigger than me, I never so much as mentioned it to anyone. But, when I woke up that morning after computer camp, with my life already in turmoil, I had a revelation: Bad stuff always happened to me because I let it. And if I was ever going to alter this course my life was on, I'd have to do something about it. So before my window screen had even stopped reverberating, I knew my oppression at the hands of Jason Cipriano had to end.

That night I set my alarm for 5:15. When I awoke, I borrowed the key to Debbie's Subaru and snuck outside to wait in the driver's seat. At 5:42 I spied Cipriano pedaling down the empty street, tossing newspapers left and right, gracefully rainbowing them onto their awaiting porches. When he got to the front of my house, he skidded his bike to a stop and lowered the kickstand. He took off the shoulder satchel that held his yet-to-be-delivered papers. He pretended to read signs from an imaginary catcher, shaking off the first two before settling on the third. Then he did a full wind up, including a Fernando Valenzuela leg kick, and sizzled the morning paper on a frozen rope directly at my bedroom window. The noise on the street was even louder than it was from inside.

Cipriano made a victorious fist-pump and climbed back onto his dirt bike to resume his route. That's when I sprang into action. I started the car, backed out of the driveway and began rolling down the street. Ahead, I could see Cipriano's silhouette scoot to the side of the road to make way. But instead of passing him, I pulled in behind and flicked on the brights. His legs started pistoning faster. The pace of his paper-throwing quickened.

Cromley

My bumper was maybe two feet from his back tire when I decided to start laying on the horn. This sent Cipriano into a panic. He stopped throwing papers and stood up on his pedals. By this point we were going twelve miles per hour. The whole time I was tailing him, I kept thinking, "I could mow you down, sucker. One twitch of my foot and you are permanently pavement."

You could say my goal was simply to scare the living crap out of him. And if that was it, I clearly achieved it. But, as is often the case with me, I couldn't tell when it was time to declare victory and move on.

Cipriano bunny-hopped the curb and veered into Dr. Kim's expansive and elaborately landscaped front yard. Undeterred, I wrenched the steering wheel in hot pursuit. Cipriano weaved his way through some juniper shrubs but got his front tire snagged on a sprinkler head. His limp body went sailing over the handlebars, surrounded by a swarm of undelivered papers. Right there, I should have stopped. But I didn't. In fact, I hit the gas. I was about to drive over the juniper bushes, and perhaps even Cipriano, when Debbie's Subaru ran head-on into one of the sandstone boulders that Dr. Kim had decorated his yard with. The front bumper caved. My head banged the steering wheel. The radiator sent out a spray of steam.

In the grass in front of me, illuminated by the Subaru's headlights, lay the semi-conscious body of Jason Cipriano. It was a windy morning and the stray newspapers had begun to split apart. Pages of gray newsprint blew from Dr. Kim's front yard out across the street, like smoke from a brushfire.

Ironically, the first person on the scene was Debbie's old boyfriend Ray the Cop, who was responding to the 9-1-1 call placed by Dr. Kim. An ambulance arrived and even a fire truck, but I think the fact that Ray was there first helped to limit the amount of trouble I got into, especially from a legal standpoint. Instead of getting arrested, I was remanded to St. Vincent's for psychological evaluation.

The Last Good Halloween

You can go ahead and add that evaluation to the long list of tests I've failed, because whatever I told them it was enough to get committed to the juvenile psych-ward, known around town as Four-North because it occupies the fourth floor of the hospital's north tower. Among the many indignities I had to endure there was the fact that they'd only allow me to wear shoes with Velcro straps, since shoelaces are apparently a common suicide tool. I really hate Velcro shoes. They stopped being cool six years ago.

In general, Four-North residents tended to keep to themselves. We'd walk around the hallways with our heads down, hoping to not be recognized. All of us – even the ones who were genuinely screwed up – were cognizant enough to know that if word got out we'd spent time there, we'd be branded for life.

If you doubt me on this, I give you the sad case of George Hanser. Three years ago, in junior high, a rumor started circulating that George had had sex with a dog. A ridiculous rumor, I'm sure, with probably zero basis in reality. Yet from that time henceforth, his nickname has been Dog-Fucker – not anything creative, just Dog-Fucker. Even *I* call him that and I'm essentially a serf in the feudal social hierarchy. I guarantee you twenty, thirty years down the line at class reunions and what-not, he'll show up with a wife and kids, maybe he's a CEO of a Fortune 500 company, and people'll be all, "Hey, Dog-Fucker, how's it going?"

None of us wanted it to be known that we were guests in Four-North. For me, this was made easier to conceal by the fact that I don't have any close friends, which means no one to betray me. It also helps that Cipriano goes to the Catholic high school, which is hermetically sealed socially from the public schools.

While I was there, I had to meet with Dr. Byrne twice a day to discuss my "feelings of anger." I thought about blaming the whole thing on video games, but Debbie never even sprang for an Atari, so I knew that was a non-starter. Whenever I told Dr. Byrne about what Cipriano had been doing with the newspapers, he kept steering things back to Debbie and Bradley and Uncle Harley and Ray and Cullen and Steven and Frank and Nick. Eventually, I figured out his game. I made sure to pepper my comments with buzzwords like "abandonment" and "awareness" and "acceptance" and "growth." Dr. Byrne started talking about how much progress I was making.

After four weeks, they gave me back my regular shoes and let me go home. Life's been different since The Event, as I call it. Debbie and I had exactly one conversation about it the day after I got back. She didn't ask me why I did it or where she'd gone wrong as a mother – she'd used the time I'd been gone to steel herself against such operatics. Instead, she told me, in no uncertain terms, that I had two strikes against me, and if I got one more I'd be sent to a place called the Haverford Military Institute in Bismarck, North Dakota. She even showed me the brochure, I guess to make the threat feel more concrete.

"Debbie, do you realize what Cipriano's been doing to me for years? Do you have any idea who's the real victim here?"

She calmly raised her hand to stop me. "I don't have any say in the matter," she said. "It was a deal I made with the police. That's the only reason you're not in jail right now."

This sounded specious, but I couldn't prove she was bluffing. Debbie then went on to detail how things were going to operate from here on out. Strict amounts of study time, closely monitored TV watching, diligent adherence to curfews (not like I ever went out), and a whole new set of household chores. All of this was non-negotiable. She even made me shake on it.

After that, we haven't spoken of The Event again. In fact, she's gone out of her way to act normal around me in the week and a half I've been home, perhaps in the hopes that I won't see myself as stigmatized by it.

During that same time, Uncle Harley and I have diligently avoided being caught alone in the same room together. The act of remaining entirely separate from someone you live with, especially in a house this size, has required some serious effort. And all the near-encounters have been the undercard to this morning's unavoidable main event: breakfast.

The fact is, I kind of liked the guy when he lived across the street and paid me to mow his lawn. Uncle Harley was the interesting bachelor who I wouldn't have minded modeling my life after. He had a decent two-bedroom house. He drives a classic Datsun 280ZX. He's got a job at the sugar beet refinery that requires him to wear a hard-hat, yet also a jacket and tie, which seems like a nice blend of both blue and white collar. And he's always had an impressive string of attractive women visiting him. They would often sunbathe on his back deck, and I would secretly spy on them when I was supposed to be mowing, and one time one of the women was topless, which was something that will shoot a man's esteem pretty high in the eyes of a kid who's never even made out with a girl before.

Of course, now that he's moved into my house, there's no denying that I'm predisposed to see his less appealing attributes. As Exhibit A, you could point to the list of his obnoxious traits I've mentally tabulated.

#1. In the mornings I can hear him expectorating in the shower, which means he spits it down the drain, and while that, in and of itself, may only be a venial sin, it's also a gateway habit that could lead to peeing in the shower and possibly even worse.

#2. He clips his toenails over the toilet bowl. On its own, I have no problem with this except that he then fails to take the next obvious step and flush, leaving little yellow sickle-moons to canoe around the surface of the toilet.

#3. He's a bona fide and (as far as I can tell) unrepentant liberal. My first clue was the *Time* magazine, but I've since found several others. Most recently, I caught him walking around the house with a ratty green t-shirt that said "Not Just Peanuts" on it. As if he didn't think I'd get the Carter reference! I don't want to make unjust

Cromley

accusations, but I'm starting to think he might even be a Dukakis booster. For years this household has been comfortably ensconced in the Reagan fold, and that's the way I intend it to stay. Frankly, my concerns here go beyond the mere political. I'm worried these newly introduced leftward influences could lead to a larger, more dangerous moral subversion.

Which brings me to #4. He and Debbie spend *lots* of time in the bedroom together – and I'm not talking about going to bed early and sleeping in. I'm talking like a thirty-minute nap after dinner, or hour-long post-lunch snoozers. I'm not an idiot. I know what's going on, though I'd rather not think about it. It's not the carnality so much as the utter flagrancy of it that galls me.

This morning, Uncle Harley and I are at opposite ends of the breakfast table, both silently leaning over our cereal in the semidarkness of an early autumn morning, when I look up and decide on one more item to add to my list:

#5. He comes to breakfast wearing only pajama bottoms. No shirt. How am I supposed to eat when confronted by his silver dollar-sized nipples and the wooly pelt of his chest? I mean, Christ, I'm forty-five minutes away from being a sophomore in high school and I've barely gotten my first real, visible pubes.

"How'd you sleep last night?"

It takes me a moment to realize it was Uncle Harley who said this.

"What kind of a question is that?" I ask.

"Sometimes an adjustment like we're going through can play havoc on the sleep cycle." He eyes me for a moment. "You look tired."

"I slept great," I assure him.

This is not entirely true. Last night I dreamed that Bradley had fallen down a well, so I took a shovel and started digging. After a few feet, though, the hole started filling up with water. The more I dug, the muddier it got, until I was neck deep in water the consistency of a chocolate milkshake. I woke up with my teeth clenched and my bed sheets soaked with sweat a half hour before my alarm was supposed to go off.

"You know, Kirby, off the record, I never liked that Jason Cipriano kid." He looks down into his bowl where a few life-rafts of Cheerios are still clinging to the edges. "I wasn't happy you did it, and you were probably acting out because of me, but I do think he had it coming."

It's an interesting maneuver, one I was not expecting. "I think my psychiatrist would be awfully disappointed to hear about the mixed messages I'm getting at home."

Uncle Harley seems to think about this, then smiles and nods. "You're a pretty smart kid," he says.

"Trust me, I'm not. And I've got a laundry list of Iowa Basic test results and one PSAT score to back me up on that. They'll basically tell you I know a few big words and that's about it."

"Maybe you got low scores because you've never applied yourself," he offers.

This sounds dangerously close to something a father is supposed to say, and I'm momentarily taken aback.

"Besides," Uncle Harley says, "I think knowing a lot of smart words can make you smart."

I pause for a moment to let that one sink in. Then I pounce, "That statement says a lot more about you than it does me."

His stare goes hard and he shifts his lips to the side. I do not yet know how to read his facial cues, although if I had to guess, I'd say he's trying to decide between busing his bowl to the sink and writing this conversation off as a loss, or engaging me further to find out precisely what kind of devil-spawn he's dealing with here.

He sets his spoon down carefully and rests his fingertips on the table. "You're a pretty wormy little shit, aren't you?" he asks.

To say I'm shocked would be an understatement. Confrontational profanity is a risky gambit so early in his tenure.

Cromley

"Uncle Harley, I hope that's not the kind of language they're teaching you down at the sugar beet refinery."

"I want you to know I get what's happening. For the record, I'd hoped it wouldn't be like this." He smiles half-heartedly. "But I guess clichés become clichés because they're true."

He leans back in his chair and angles a hairy forearm on the edge of the table. "Seems like a pretty clear-cut Oedipal Complex going on here."

"I'm only a sophomore," I say. "We don't read *Oedipus Rex* 'til later this year."

"But you're familiar with the concept, yes?"

"Basically a guy loves his mother. Kills his father. Gets married. Blah, blah, blah."

"That's about right," he says, nodding. "You think that's what's going on, or am I just full of Cheerios?"

"Since I haven't read the source text, and I never knew my real father, and I had nothing to do with my stepfather's disappearance, and I don't intend to start dating Debbie any time in the near future, it'd be hard to sign off on the comparison."

"As someone who *has* read it, I can tell you it strongly pertains to your current state of mind."

"Is that some kind of reference to Velcro shoes?" I ask, suddenly defensive.

Uncle Harley looks lost for a moment. He must not know about that detail of my stay at Four-North.

"I'll talk with Dr. Byrne about that at our next appointment," I say. "Until then, I'll provisionally take your word for it."

Mercifully, Debbie comes into the room like a referee to put an end to the sparring session. She's running a brush through her shower-moist hair. A light breeze of Dove moisturizer trails behind her.

"Good morning, boys," she says. Uncle Harley and I both lower our guards and return to our respective corners.

The Last Good Halloween

Debbie works part-time at an art gallery downtown called The Peacock. It specializes in Western art, which she hates, but it's the only kind that sells around here. She also works part-time at a pawnshop on Montana Avenue. She's wearing lots of rhinestones and turquoise this morning, so today she must be working at The Peacock. The days she's at the pawnshop, she usually wears black rock concert t-shirts and tight jeans.

"Kirby, come on, sweetie, we've got to get going."

"It takes ten minutes to walk to school. I've got, like, a half hour."

"It's, *like*, the first day of school," she says, apparently mocking a tone I've just taken, but which I'm pretty sure doesn't sound like me.

"That's not very funny," I say, "nor accurate."

"You know I don't take tradition lightly, Kirby."

Out of the corner of my eye, I catch Uncle Harley absorbing this exchange with a satisfied grin. He's rightly surmised that whatever tradition Debbie's referring to, it's not one I'm fond of.

"Debbie, maybe this is the year – what with all the changes going on – we ought to bury this old tradition. It's kind of anachronistic at this point, don't you think?"

She stops brushing mid-swipe so her hair is standing straight up under the tension of the bristles. I notice a slight heave that starts somewhere in her womb, works its way up her torso and reaches its terminus as a twitch in her right eyelid.

"I've been taking you to the first day of school for the last eleven years. I've got basically this year and two more left after it." Her eyes are watery, brimming. "Do you really want to deny your mother this small pleasure so close to the end?"

Hell yes! is what I *should* say. After all, part of the reason my life is so middling is precisely because I'm too big of a pushover, too easily corralled into staying in line. And yet, it's my mom. Seeing her there, on the verge of tears that will certainly wreck her makeup and force her into a lengthy retouching session, I find myself unable to pull the trigger.

"Let me get my coat," I say. It kills me how soft I am. Maybe I do have an Oedipal Complex.

Debbie's face bends into a dim half-smile that tells me her victory wasn't quite worth the cost. "I'll be out at the car," she says. "Don't drag like you do."

Outside, I decide to take a gamble.

"You know, Debbie, technically, *I* could drive us to school."

Debbie looks at me, then at the dented bumper on her car. It's true I did manage to get my learner's permit before computer camp, but ever since The Event, driving is a touchy subject.

"Get in the car, mister," she says.

Uncle Harley was right about me knowing a bunch of big words. That comes from a strange childhood phase when I only liked to read vocabulary-builder books. While everyone else was blowing through *Narnia* or *A Wrinkle in Time* or *Where the Red Fern Grows*, I was learning what *exegesis* and *visceral* mean. There's no way for me to explain this perverse fascination, though I can tell you that ever since procuring *The Art of Nude Photography*, I'd much rather jerk off than learn what *solipsistic* means – so I can't be too abnormal. Also, I wasn't kidding about what I said about being smart. I'm not. By every measure out there – grades, test scores, teacher reports – I am a person of average intelligence. But I know the big vocabulary can be deceptive. In seventh grade they even yanked me out of class and made me take one of those under-achieving-genius tests to see if I was doing so badly in school on account of being too smart. I remember one of the questions they asked was what salt and water had in common. I said neither was an ingredient in candy. They didn't stick me in any kind of gifted program afterwards, so I figure they found no hints of brilliance.

"I see you inching down in your seat, young man," Debbie says.

The Last Good Halloween

"I was thinking," I say. "Any inching taking place was a result of deep thought."

She's got a Rolling Stones tape playing "Undercover of the Night." Debbie's love of classic rock is a holdover from our year with Steven the DJ.

"You sure seem embarrassed."

"Well, I'm not."

"It's awfully uninspired to be embarrassed of your mother, Kirby. You're more original than that."

"I'm not embarrassed to be seen with you, Debbie. Okay? I love it!"

She smiles, a sign that her needling had been done with the purpose of producing the exact reaction she just got. Aside from that, though, I sense something buoyant about her this morning. Ever since negotiating the driveway back-out, she's got this holding-her-breath look like she's trying to stop herself from saying something.

"Is everything all right?" I ask.

"Surely, Shirley," she says. The Subaru is creeping along at fifteen MPH because this is a park zone. She giggles, then starts tapping her index fingers on the top of the steering wheel as if she were playing "Chopsticks."

"I don't even know how to say it," she says at last. "I'm just so..."

A frisson of dread mounts inside the car as I await her word selection. Though the Bradley-Returns Index isn't technically at zero, it's about as low as it can be while the man still has a pulse.

"...so, so...happy." She giggles again as we pull up to the stoplight. This was possibly the worst adjectival outcome as far as the BRI is concerned and will necessitate some immediate pushback if I'm going to contain the damage.

"You know, Debbie," I say, trying to sound as sober as possible, "this has all happened awfully fast. I mean, how well do you really know this Uncle Harley character?"

Cromley

"What do you mean?"

"Nothing specifically. It's just that replacing Bradley so quickly, it seems kind of rushed. I know the man had his faults, but he was stable. And I think that that stability has allowed us to thrive on certain not-obvious, but important levels."

The light turns green and Debbie eases into the intersection, left turn signal a-clicking. Whatever bubble of giddiness she'd been floating in has been popped and now it's all-business Debbie. "Sweetie, I don't think you understand how unhappy I was with Bradley the last couple years."

"Yes, but don't you think maybe because of the new glow Uncle Harley gives off that's making Bradley seem dim by comparison? And maybe, given time, he could end up being more of a dud than Bradley?"

"You make a good point," she says. "I'm a heart-person, lead with my emotions. Always have. You're more like your father."

Hearing reference to the Original Biological Contributor fills me with an unpleasant queasiness.

"Do you even know where Bradley is right now?"

"I don't." Her lips are pressed together tightly as she says this – possibly a sign of subterfuge, though I can't be sure.

"If he comes back and sees what's going on, the man is liable to go postal."

A gap opens up in the traffic and she guns the car through the turn.

"That man doesn't have a violent bone in his body," she says. "Besides, I doubt he'd be jealous. It's been a long time since he's been a real husband to your mother."

She's steering the conversation onto a path I can't follow – especially now that Uncle Harley said I might have an Oedipal Complex. This tete-a-tete needs a serious shakeup if anything productive is going to come out of it.

The Last Good Halloween

"Mom," I say, my tone grave, "I had a bad dream about Bradley. A really bad one."

Debbie eases onto the brakes because we're already pulling up to the front of school. She looks at me, a fearful tremble in her eyes. She tends to assign outsized importance to dreams, so I had a feeling this revelation would hold some cachet.

"A bad dream?" she asks.

"Yeah, he was in trouble and needed help."

She looks out the window and scans the front of the school, even though she doesn't appear to be looking for anything in particular.

"I want you to forget that dream, all right? It doesn't mean a thing. Or it might mean the opposite, that he's doing really well."

She looks back at me and brightens her face. "Now, here we are. Your first day as a sophomore. This is your year, kiddo. Good things are on the way, right over the next horizon. The world is going to know who Kirby Russo is this year."

"Careful what you wish for," I say, then reach for the door handle.

"Excuse me, sir," Debbie says. "You know you can't leave 'til I get my kiss."

I turn back to her. She's smiling expectantly. If I refuse her – the simple, thoughtless gesture of a callow boy – she'll be devastated. Why would you ever allow yourself to be put in such a vulnerable position? It makes no sense.

"Let's do a hug," I suggest.

I detect an emotional tremor gaining purchase somewhere deep inside her. So I lean back across the front seat, leave a dry peck on my mother's cheek and claw at the door handle before anyone walking past can place me in the car.

"Have a wonderful first day, darling," she calls out before I've got the door closed.

Cromley

The Subaru pulls away behind me as I stand shoulders-squared before the dull brick façade of Roosevelt High. I take in a deep, calming breath the way Dr. Byrne taught me to and bury my shaking hands in my pockets. How could Debbie know the real reason I was inching down in my seat?

Inside, the terrazzo floors are polished within an inch of their lives. It's still a little early and the hallways aren't yet packed. As I make my way to my locker, I don't notice anything unusual – no gawking or finger pointing. Maybe no one knows where I spent the second half of the summer; it's conceivable my secret remains intact.

When I get to my locker, though, I'm shattered. Just below the gill slits on the door, someone's taken a sharp object and etched one word into the brown paint: PSYCHO.

Panic-stricken, I look up and down the hallway. No one seems to be watching. No snickering hyenas. I fish around in my backpack until I find a magic marker. Then I doctor the letters so they read: TIPSY-CHOICE.

Who knows what it's supposed to mean? It's the best I can do on the spot, and it'll probably suffice. Still, this only masks the larger problem: Someone out there knows about Four-North and the Velcro shoes, and they even know the nickname they want to give me.

Chapter 3

It's been two weeks since school started, and I haven't picked up any other hints that someone knows about The Event. It's possible the graffito on my locker was a random act of vandalism. After all, if my secret was going to come out, it probably would've already happened. But I'm not ready to start breathing easy. I'm still tip-toeing past the graveyard.

At 10:31 Mr. Gorton, my third period typing teacher, lumbers in. He stands at the head of the classroom and sweeps his eyes slowly from front to back. Mr. Gorton has the build of Frankenstein's monster, minus the neck bolts. Two days ago on the way to school, I cut through the faculty parking lot and saw him in his car smoking a big Sherlock Holmes pipe. I think what struck me most was seeing his giant frame folded up into a Ford Fiesta driver's seat. When he saw me watching him, he got a guilty look on his face, as if I'd just caught him doing something wrong. Since then, I get the sense he doesn't quite trust me, like I've made it onto his personal watch list.

"Okay, class, we're going to start off with a timed quiz. Turn to page 81." His voice is absurdly low and slow, like a sound your Walkman makes when the batteries are almost dead. "Line up your paper over the barrel of the typewriter and scroll down eight lines."

The Last Good Halloween

I glance to my left because a set of black fingernails is already silently pecking the keys of the machine next to mine. The typewriters in this classroom are equipped with a tiny word processing screen. If you set it to that mode, you can type the entire first line of text before the quiz starts. When Mr. Gorton says go, you hit return and the machine hammers it out at lightning speed; then you switch back to normal typing mode with a full-line head start. I've never taken advantage of this loophole – not because I'm a strict adherent to the honor code, but rather because I've decided, given my limited intelligence, the ability to type could very well be the difference between gainful employment and the breadline. The owner of the black fingernails next to me does not feel the same way.

They belong to a junior named Izzy Woodley. Last year, we were both in the same orchestra class. I struggled with the timpani until our teacher realized my talents lay outside the musical realm and made it clear I should quit orchestra to find out what they were. Izzy, on the other hand, played viola and was actually good – like maybe first chair or something. I remember, though, she abruptly quit halfway through the first semester. Nowadays, I sometimes see her sitting on a circle of picnic benches in Prospect Park where she and a lot of other black-clothed juveniles smoke cigarettes and loiter menacingly.

She catches me eyeing her busy fingers and shoots me a look.

"I don't usually cheat," she whispers.

We've been sitting next to each other since the beginning of school. This is the first thing she's said to me, and it's a lie.

"I know," I whisper back.

"I'm messed up today," she says.

Upon closer inspection, her pupils are dilated, and they're jumping left and right in a way that would be hard to do voluntarily.

"I'm sorry to hear that," I say

"Imagine every inch of your skin is covered by spiders."

Cromley

"I'd rather not."

"That's what mine feels like right now." She nods as if she's proven a point. "You'd want a head start on your typing quiz too."

At the front of the room, Mr. Gorton raises his hands as if he's about to conduct a symphony. "Ready... And... Begin."

Izzy splotches the return key with her pinkie and the carriage goes sailing across the page. Mr. Gorton hears someone's typewriter hammering far faster than any of us novices are capable of and begins marching down the aisle searching for the culprit. By the time he gets to our row, Izzy's got her machine switched back over to normal mode. But he lingers over my shoulder, which is a little like having a gorilla with smoker's breath mouth-breathing in your ear. The whole thing makes me nervous and causes me to accidentally transpose the F and G keys so my fourth line reads: `The thinf is Grank wants us to do a food job in the fallery.`

When Mr. Gorton calls time, he has us count up the number of words and errors and run them through a formula that tells us our grade. My results yield a D, worse than usual on account of the unforced errors. Izzy's, I notice, is a B plus.

"Typing's my best class," she says after we've passed our quizzes forward.

Her hair is coarse and black, though it's more of a dark brown at the roots. Her bangs fall unevenly above her eyebrows. The whole look seems intentionally amateurish – a big departure from the other girls at Roosevelt who are chiefly concerned with the creation of hair-tsunamis frozen mid-crest over their foreheads.

"What are you on?" I ask her. It's a bold question, especially since we've never spoken before today.

She glances up at Mr. Gorton, who's sitting behind his desk, poring over the quizzes, perhaps trying to deduce which one was typed by the cheater. In a moment, he'll give up and assign some busy work from the textbook.

The Last Good Halloween

She leans in toward me. "I smoked some shoe rubber," she whispers.

"Actual shoe rubber?"

She shrugs. "It's probably just the street-name."

"You smoked something that might or might not have been the bottom of someone's shoe?"

She stifles a giggle with her fingertips. "Isn't that messed up, Kirby?"

I'm momentarily stunned. Someone I've never spoken to, someone I have nothing in common with other than one class, knows my name. And she's female! This is a first.

"Does the buzz feel good at least?" I ask. Drugs are not my forte, so I'm not sure if *buzz* is a proper, or contemporary, drug expression.

She shakes her head and claws at her arms, leaving red zigzags on the flesh. "Talking about it makes it worse."

"Oh," I say, "sorry."

Our conversation appears to be in danger of stalling out when she manages to pop its clutch with, "I see you some mornings. You walk through the park."

"We used to be in orchestra together. I wasn't very good. You probably don't remember."

A troubled look crosses her face. "What's your story?"

Maybe it's due to my initial success with the straightforward approach, or maybe it's because I haven't told anyone other than Julian and I really, really need to spill what's on my mind to someone who might have an idea what I should do – whatever the cause, I blurt: "Bradley's skipped town and Uncle Harley's moved in and he's making himself right at home in all sorts of nasty ways."

"Whoa," she says. "Is that a soap opera you watch?"

"No, it's real life. Bradley's my step-dad. He left town. Uncle Harley's not my real uncle. He's my neighbor. Except he's not my neighbor anymore because he's moved in and my mom and him are together now."

She cracks the knuckles on her left hand. "S'fucked up," she says.

Unable to find the cheater, Mr. Gorton stands up from his desk. "Now, turn to page 95 in your books and complete exercises 2 and 3." He starts to sit, but pauses halfway down and looks in my direction. "And I don't want any more talking."

Our conversation is over before it could actually bear fruit. Dutifully, we incline our heads and begin pecking away at our keyboards.

A while later, an elbow nudges my arm. Izzy clears her throat and nods toward her paper in the typewriter.

It says: `You should kill him.`

Thrown off, I hit return on mine and type: `Who?`

She clacks: `Uncle Harley.`

I shake my head, confused.

She types: `Your situation is just like Hamlet. You have to kill your uncle.`

I type: `I haven't read Hamtel.`

She types: `It might help.`

I type: `How would you know? Hamlet's not til senior year. You"re a junior.`

She types: `There's no law you can't read Hamlet on your own.` She pauses, then hits return and adds: `Don't wait like Hamlet did. Uncle Harley has to die.`

I type: `Gulp.`

The bell in the hallway rings. "Okay, students, that's all for today," Mr. Gorton intones. "Remove your exercises from the machines and hand them in as you leave."

Izzy and I take out our papers. We wad them up and stuff them in our pockets before we reach the front of the room. Neither of us will get credit for today's work.

The Last Good Halloween

I'm headed toward my locker, one tiny molecule amid all the other molecules, half on their way to lunch, half headed to their next class.

Roosevelt High – named after the earthy outdoorsman Ted, and not the effete East Coaster Frank – is, in my view, a perfect example of the typical American public high school. It's not some elite private prep thing and it's not some falling-down urban nightmare. The kids come from a wide mix of incomes and, for the most part, receive a totally serviceable education inside these walls. On some level, you can take pride in its complete and utter averageness. I know I do.

I'm just spinning the dial on my locker when Julian materializes at my left shoulder. He's wearing a pair of corduroy OP shorts that make his pale legs look like toothpicks. He's got Top-Siders on with ankle socks.

"You ready for lunch?" he asks. "I'm starving."

I see him glance at the TIPSY-CHOICE on my locker. He hasn't yet asked me about it, but I don't consider him a suspect. He was away at church camp during most of my stay at Four-North. Besides, if he really knew about The Event, he wouldn't be hanging out with me.

"Hey, Julian, you haven't read *Hamlet*, have you?"

"*Hamlet*'s not 'til senior year," he says.

"I thought so."

"Freshmen read *Romeo and Juliet* and *Macbeth*, except for Mrs. Field's class which substitutes *Midsummer Night's Dream* for *Macbeth* because she's a pacifist. And, yeah—"

He bites his words off abruptly, though I know where he was headed. Last year, when his mother found out he was reading *Midsummer Night's Dream*, she filed a protest with the school board because she said it represented anti-Christian values. They finally resolved the dispute by transferring him out of Mrs. Field's class and into Mr. Hackert's.

Cromley

"You don't have a copy of it, do you?"

"I told you. It's not 'til senior year," he says. "Why?"

"No reason. Just curious."

The students who were headed to class are gone now and the only ones left are, like us, migrating toward the cafeteria.

"Who gets curious about *Hamlet*?" he asks.

"You know, Julian, it's possible that literature can actually inform you about the human condition. It's possible it could reveal some truth about life."

I'm about to continue my defense of literature and maybe even slip in a shot at his family's over-the-top Christianity when I happen to notice Mr. Corey, my English teacher, pass through the stairwell heading upstairs.

"To be continued," I say, slamming my locker closed and moving past him.

"Where are you going?"

"I'll meet you in the cafeteria."

I catch up to Mr. Corey by the time he's reached the third floor.

"Mr. Corey," I huff breathlessly. "Kirby Russo, from your fifth period English."

I reach my hand out towards him and the gesture seems to catch him off-guard because all he does is look at my hand and then back up at my face. Mr. Corey has waxy red hair and a matching mustache. He's been an assistant coach on the football team forever, and rumor has it he's next in line for the top job if the team has one more losing season. Teaching is what he does to support his coaching habit.

"What do you need, Kirby?" He resumes marching down the hallway.

"I just wanted to check which Shakespeare plays we'd be reading in class this year."

"It's sophomore year," he says matter-of-factly, "so *Julius Caesar*."

The Last Good Halloween

"Just one?"

We've reached his classroom. He stops and turns before opening the door. "We're also doing *Antigone* and *Oedipus Rex*, so there's no time for another Shakespeare play." He reaches for the keys clipped to his belt loop.

"I admit I'm interested in *Oedipus*," I say, "for personal reasons."

"Okay then, I'll see you—"

"But would it be possible to vote for *Hamlet*?"

He stops moving the keys toward the door. His mustache twitches in a way that signifies, at once, annoyance and threat.

"In case you're taking requests."

"It's school, Kirby. Not a democracy."

"Sure, but maybe just this once—"

"You can't read *Hamlet* 'til you're a senior."

"Why not?"

He pauses for a moment to consider this. "Because it's too mature for sophomores," he says. "Now, if you'll let me get—"

"Mr. Corey, it's clear, judging from my height and build, that I will never be a member of your football team, and, thus, merit only a minimum of your time or attention. But still, I'm asking you these questions in earnest, and I'd appreciate it if you'd at least consider my request."

He leans down toward me and I catch a whiff of overly strong aftershave. "You're a smart kid, Kirby."

"Actually, I'm not."

"But angry."

I don't bother to deny this second assertion because Dr. Byrne and Jason Cipriano would probably agree.

Mr. Corey's lips curl up into a sly grin at the edges. "By the way, son, I noticed some graffiti on your locker the other day. What does TIPSY-CHOICE mean?"

Cromley

My mouth goes dry. My cheek muscles go slack. "I think it's a street gang," I say.

"A *street* gang? How is that different from a *gang*-gang?"

"They're trying to recruit me. That's why they tagged my locker. Maybe reading *Hamlet* will help me learn the value of education and keep me on the right path." I can hear the panic in my own voice. It must be obvious to him.

"I've never heard of the Tipsy-Choicers before," he says, leaning back.

"Oh, they're pretty cutthroat."

Mr. Corey nods. His eyelids are two narrow slits. He doesn't believe me, but he doesn't have the energy to pursue it either.

"Wait a minute." He unlocks his door and enters the classroom. When he returns, he hands me a flimsy paperback. "I want this returned by the end of the quarter," he says.

In my hands is a dog-eared copy of *Hamlet*. It's so light and puny. How come everyone's making such a big deal over something so insubstantial?

School is out and I'm hiking north through the student parking lot when I hear someone calling my name. It's Julian, saddled with an overstuffed backpack that makes him look distinctly turtle-like.

I contemplate pretending to not hear him and hoofing onwards, but I feel bad for abandoning him at lunch earlier today. So I wait as he double-times it to catch up.

Julian lives directly east of Prospect Park, whereas I live north and east. So we can walk together for one leg, provided I don't take the hypotenuse route. The temperature has been dropping all day and it now feels like it's dipping into the forties. The leaves on the trees overhead make a clapping noise when the wind blows, as if the chlorophyll in their veins had already frozen.

As we walk, I can see Julian's nearly bare legs are grayish-pink and dappled with goosebumps. I have to wonder how his mom let him leave the house this morning in shorts. Is this a meteorological miscue in the Miller household, or perhaps is it negligence of a more systemic variety? Something's going wrong there. I don't know what, but something.

"Hey, Julian, does your church let you guys read weather forecasts?"

He tucks his thumbs under his backpack straps. "Very funny."

"Who's trying to be funny?"

He's looking at the sidewalk carefully, as if he wants to be sure each foot lands on solid ground.

"Julian, do you mind if I ask you something?"

He doesn't say anything.

"What's it like to have a real family?" I'm not sure why I ask him this, other than I guess I'd really like to know the answer.

"Ha ha, Kirby. Very funny again."

"I wasn't joking this time," I admit. "What's a real family like?"

We walk a few more paces in silence. Then Julian stops and turns toward me. "I don't know what a real family is," he says.

"Sure you do. Normal mother, biological father, decent house. I don't have any of those."

"I see what you mean." A breeze kicks up and he jams his hands into his shorts pockets. "I think it's easy for something to look normal from the outside," he says. "Trust me, even a family like mine can be pretty messed-up on the inside."

With that, we go our separate ways.

Since leaving Julian I've counted five Bush yard signs and two for Dukakis, a ratio that bodes well, I believe. When I reach the northeast corner of the park, I see Uncle Harley's old house, with its forlorn For Sale By Owner sign staked in the front yard. I'm half-tempted to transplant one of the Bush signs into his yard just to see what happens, but I'm eager to get home now, so I'll have to put that one on my to-do list.

Cromley

A brown UPS van rumbles past and I'm about to cross Cherrybrook Drive when I notice a parked Chevy Lumina whose driver is staring intently at our front door.

I stop in my tracks, unsure what to do. Confront or hide? Fight or flight? As I weigh the merits of both approaches, the guy in the Lumina looks over and sees me watching him.

He's got scruffy blond hair that's long in the back and a ragged flannel shirt with a puffy down vest. His eyes follow me while I cross the street. As soon as I turn up the front walkway to my house, he unrolls his window and leans out.

"You live there, kid?"

I notice he's wearing leather gloves. Any time I see someone wearing gloves for no apparent reason I get nervous because I always think they might be planning to do something they don't want to leave fingerprints for.

"If you imagine I'm going to tell you where I live you must be some kind of idiot," I say.

The guy chuckles humorlessly and leans on the open window sill. He's got the forearms of a plumber.

"Are you one of Uncle Harley's grubby friends?" I ask, because this seems like the likeliest scenario.

"I'm looking for Brad Kellogg," he says. "Does he live there?"

It's been a while since anyone's mentioned his name around here. Just hearing it uttered by a complete stranger is enough to give the Bradley-Returns Index a flutter of life. Then again, this guy worries me. Based on appearances, I'd say he looks scuzzy, maybe even dangerous.

"Is Bradley in some kind of trouble?" I ask.

The man looks up and down the street. "Depends on what you mean by trouble."

I'm standing close enough to the car now that I can see inside. The passenger seat and floorboards are covered with wadded-up fast food wrappers and Mountain Dew bottles.

The Last Good Halloween

"Does he owe you money or something?"

The man's eyes are the glacial blue of a husky, yet there's something strangely lifeless in them.

"You could say that," he says.

Right then I decide this is not a good man, and, if anything, Bradley needs to be shielded from him.

"That dirtbag hasn't been here in months," I say. "We've moved on. So if you're looking for him, you're out of luck."

The man in the car doesn't say anything, just keeps his gaze settled on me. I take one step closer, careful not to breach the perimeter wherein he might conceivably be able to reach out and grab me.

"Why don't you take that piece of shit car and drive your ass out of here?"

If I weren't a kid, he'd probably get out and beat me senseless. And I can tell he's contemplating that course of action right now. But I *am* a kid, so, for a little while longer at least, I can get away with saying stuff like that to adults. I stand there on the sidewalk with my hip cocked. I wait until he starts his engine and roars off down Cherrybrook Drive.

It's only after he's out of sight that I wobble over to the juniper shrubs and vomit what's left of lunch.

Once I've gathered myself, I pull open the front door. Fortunately, the only one home is Mr. T. He scurries up and sniffs me eagerly, his stumpy tail quivering back and forth, moist beard tickling my ankles. As a schnauzer, Mr. T is the surliest dog I've ever known. He is fiercely loyal to me and no one else – not Debbie, not Bradley, and certainly not Uncle Harley.

He's found some smell he likes on my shoes and it's sending him into a snorting frenzy. But I nudge him away because I'm in serious need of some R&R right now. My intention is to make myself a cocktail and spend a little quality time in my bedroom with *The Art of Nude Photography*. Then, maybe I'll microwave some egg rolls and begin to contemplate what this creepy visitor means as it pertains to the BRI.

"Come on, boy," I say, heading toward the back door. "You look like you need a little fresh air."

For some reason he's not buying it, so I have to drag him by the collar across the floor. When I get the door open, I see Uncle Harley digging near the back fence with a shovel. He sees me out of the corner of his eye and waves me over. Mr. T uses this chance to make a break for the living room, so I head out alone. Uncle Harley's got a ten-by-ten patch of yard de-sodded, and he's breaking up the dirt chunks with the shovel blade.

"What's the meaning of all this?" I ask.

"It's a shame to let this big yard go to waste," he says.

"I *was* thinking of having a basketball court put in there."

He wipes his face with the back of his hand. "This spring we're going to plant ourselves an organic vegetable garden."

"What the hell does *organic* mean?"

"No pesticides. No fertilizer. No artificial chemicals. Just plain old natural vegetables."

I take this as further evidence of his liberal tendencies and another reason not to trust him. "You are aware of the army worm situation around these parts every summer, aren't you?"

"It might take a little extra work," he says. "But the rewards'll be worth it."

"Why didn't you ever have a garden in your *own* yard?"

He claps his hands together to knock the excess dirt off. "Everything is always improving," he says, smiling. "All of us are always getting better."

I'd like nothing more than to pick apart this Pollyanna tripe, but I get the sense that that might be part of the game he's playing. So instead I try to catch him off guard with:

"I saw a pretty funny picture of Dukakis in the paper the other day."

The Last Good Halloween

Harley picks up the shovel and begins turning the soil again. "Oh yeah?"

"He was riding around in some tank. He's got a helmet on his head, and he looks like a jack-o-lantern."

Uncle Harley grimaces, or at least I think that's what he does. It's hard to tell what he's doing behind that Captain Caveman beard.

"What do you have against Dukakis?" he asks.

"For me, it's all about the taxes. If he gets the chance, he's going to turn this whole country into Taxachusetts."

Harley casts a glance my way without turning his shoulders. "And you think Bush is going to be so much better on that front?"

"You heard what he said at the convention: 'Read my lips...'"

"What do you know about taxes, Kirby? You haven't paid a tax in your life."

"Yes, but my caregivers pay taxes all the time. So I pay taxes by proxy."

He nods at this, though not in agreement.

"Plus, I'm too young to vote. Which is tantamount to taxation without representation."

"Jeez, Kirby," he says, "I had no idea how hard you've had it all these years."

I've got him wound up a little; now's the time to find out what he knows. "Hey, you wouldn't know where Bradley is, would you?"

Uncle Harley stops working.

"You might remember him. Almost six feet. Brown hair. Used to sleep here."

"Nope." He shakes his head, trying to be nonchalant.

"Nope, you don't know where he is? Or nope, you don't remember him?"

"Why are you asking me this, Kirby?"

"It's not just me," I assure him. "People are starting to ask questions around here."

Cromley

Uncle Harley looks at me a moment. "I have no idea where the man is." He wipes his face with his sleeve and spears the shovel into the topsoil so that it stands up on its own. Then he takes off his gardening gloves and passes me on his way inside the house.

What a doofus. The man is completely oblivious to the fact that there are strange men prowling around asking questions about his predecessor. I'm not going to put *Home Protector* on his list of job titles any time soon. And tonight I'm sleeping with a baseball bat next to my bed.

Chapter 4

Believe it or not, I've got a pretty good idea what my real problem is. If I'm not careful, I can kind of slip off the normal track and get too focused on one small side-thing, to the point where I think only about that side-thing to the exclusion of all the other things that also need my attention. Sometimes it can freak people out when I'll bring something up that I've been obsessing about but no one else has mentioned for two weeks.

For the record, though, this sidetrack thing isn't all bad. It does occasionally allow me the kind of deep, impenetrable focus that Buddhist monks are said to attain after years of meditation. And if the side-thing I'm focusing on is worthwhile (a big and uncontrollable *if*) I can get pretty proficient at it. For example, the whole phase I went through where I couldn't stop reading vocabulary-builder books ultimately led me to have a pretty sweet vocabulary.

The point is I can feel another one of my tunnel-vision phases coming on. This one has to do with *Hamlet*, which is proving to be a more difficult read than I'd anticipated. The copy Mr. Corey gave me is one of those cheapo editions they sell in bulk, and has exactly zero annotations. Since I'm on my own to decipher all the cockeyed phrases and antiquated words, I can't get more than a few lines without having to resort to a bulky dictionary.

I'm also determined to read as much of it as possible directly in front of Debbie and Uncle Harley – just to see them squirm, though it isn't 'til I'm a good way into Act II and I bring it to dinner, that I finally get a reaction.

"Kirby, why are those books on the table?" Debbie asks as she cranes a wad of salad and deposits it on my plate.

"It's *Hamlet*," I say, as if I'm answering her question.

"I can see that," she says. "But why's it at the table? It's going to get garbaged."

I hadn't anticipated her getting caught up in the semantics of dinner table reading etiquette. "It's really *good*. Man, I can't believe how *good* it is."

She arches her eyebrows and loads a spoonful of steamed carrots. Since Uncle Harley's started squatting here, I've noticed small changes in our eating habits. The oil and vinegar salad dressing of old is now referred to as vinaigrette. And I've been introduced to something called couscous, which I don't understand the point of. Basically, it seems like Rice-A-Roni crushed into very small pieces with all the flavor drained out.

"I never liked his tragedies," Debbie says. "Too much violence for me. The comedies are more my style – give me *As You Like It* over *Hamlet* any day."

She's edging away from my conversational snare, so I counter with, "Reading Shakespeare is like holding a mirror up to life," which I stole straight from the book's skimpy foreword, and seems like a point that neither of my dinner companions will be able to ignore.

I glance over at Uncle Harley to see how he takes it. All I get is a slow nod and a flexing of his beard.

"I didn't realize they had you reading *Hamlet* as sophomores," Debbie says. She's sawing away at a tough piece of cube steak.

Cromley

"It's not for school," I say, proudly. "I'm reading this extra-curricularly."

What happens next is the fundamental thing that's wrong with Debbie, in my opinion. As soon as she hears I'm reading *Hamlet* on my own, her face sags, like it's a balloon and you could see the air just whistling right out of it.

"What about your class reading, Kirby?"

"It's some stupid Greek thing about a chick who wants to bury her dead brother. Very dull. Two thumbs down."

Debbie sets her silverware next to her plate and glances across at Uncle Harley, who seems to be absorbed in his meal. Sensing a possible meltdown of Debbie's core reactor, I focus with a newfound intensity on my steamed carrots.

"Are you keeping up on your class reading?" she asks, voice carefully modulated.

"More or less."

She's been down this path often enough to know this is code for no. "I thought we'd talked about how important it is to stay caught up in your school work. To stay focused."

"As I recall, that subject has come up in passing."

"But?" Her voice is beginning to betray her emotions now, and I'm actually surprised at how long she's held it together.

"But this just—"

"You *promised* me you'd do a better job staying focused on your schoolwork, on the things that matter."

"I'm not going to deny that promises were made, Debbie."

And that's right where I pushed it too far. She slams her hand down flat on the table. Hard – so hard the plates and silverware jump and rattle. A wave of two percent breaches the lip of my glass and begins soaking into the tablecloth. It's a good thing no tiny dinner-table village had chosen to locate itself right there because if they had, it would be a genuine tragedy. And I'm just starting to breathe a sigh of relief at this catastrophe averted, when Debbie snaps:

"Are you even listening to me?"

"Of course."

"Do you understand why I'm angry with you right now?"

I doubt the fact that I'm reading *Hamlet* outside of my school work would be enough to constitute strike three – that this would be the peccadillo that gets me packed off to military school – but it's hard to know with Debbie these days, so a little discretion is probably in order.

"Yes," I say with what I hope is appropriate meekness, "I understand."

"Can you think of what to do that might make me *less* upset?"

"Concentrate more on my school reading?"

This was the correct answer. Debbie's reactor cools and the only sound for the next couple minutes is the muted clinking of silverware as it conveys food to our mouths.

It's Uncle Harley who finally breaks the silence. "I remember *Hamlet*." He angles the bowl of carrots and bulldozes a mound onto his plate. Then he gets this faraway look. "'Madness in great ones must not unwatched go,'" he says. "End of Act Three, Scene One, if I recall."

"I'm not that far yet," I say.

"I actually think it's good to try reading *Hamlet* now," he says, leaning back in his chair. "I was forced to do it in high school and hated every second of it. Then we read it in college and it was as if I was seeing a different play. All of a sudden I loved it. Two years made all the difference."

A quick glance at Debbie's pursed lips and narrowed eyes tells me she's silently fuming over Uncle Harley's indulgence.

But he goes on. "I guess I'm saying it's good to give it a shot now, even if you don't get it. Then when you come back later, it'll be easier to understand."

Cromley

Debbie lets out an exasperated sigh, one of her many nonverbal cues which Uncle Harley has yet to learn. He sits there a moment, looking off into space, his tongue idly chasing a stray piece of food above his right canine. The big dummy has no idea the trouble he's making for himself.

He leans forward and begins mixing the couscous with the carrots.

"One thing I've noticed," I say, pausing ever so slightly for dramatic effect, "Hamlet's situation sure does seem an awful lot like my situation. Missing father. Usurping uncle."

Harley glances up from his plate. He's got this weird half-smile on his face, and I think it's a look that's either the cat that ate the canary or the cat that's just pretended to eat the canary. Without changing his expression a single degree either way, he says, "That it is, Kirby. That it is."

I don't really know what's happened, but Debbie seems to. She huffs loudly, and hisses, "This is ridiculous."

She pushes her chair back and takes her plate to the kitchen, where she sets it down extra heavily in the sink. She goes to the bedroom and slams the door.

Uncle Harley and I look at each other across the vacuum that's left behind. He frowns deeply and goes back to eating. He's still working on his food by the time I'm done, so I clear the table around him and retire to my bedroom with *Hamlet*.

I can hear him watching TV in the living room, then later I hear bickering coming from the master bedroom. When I wake up at 3:30 needing to pee, I notice the TV is back on and Uncle Harley's asleep on the couch, bathed in its warm light.

Walking to school that next morning, I'm just about to reach the student parking lot when I glance over at a ring of picnic tables situated behind a cluster of tall pine trees. Lounging on the tables is a handful of darkly clad ruffians, shrouded by a bluish cloud of smoke. This clique is known broadly as the Neo-Thrashers, since a disproportionate number of them are skateboarders. While they belong to the same genus as the Metal-Heads, Stoners, and Goths, they are distinct enough to merit their own species. If pressed, I'd say the difference lies in the fact that the Neo-Thrashers have a shred more intelligence, and their overall philosophy tends more toward anarchy.

I quickly avert my gaze and hunch my shoulders, so as not to draw any undue attention. While the Neo-Thrashers are not a particularly violent group, it's a good idea for someone like me to treat any pack of students as potential predators. I'm almost to the chain-link parking lot gate when someone from the tables calls my name. I recognize the voice as Izzy's, yet there's something lazy and indistinct about it.

When I glance over, they're all looking at me, pale faces made paler by their black clothes. Izzy's sitting on a red picnic table with her legs dangling off the edge, her feet scissoring the air.

"Hey, Kirby!" she shouts.

"Hey," I call back.

She makes a beckoning gesture. "Hey, Kirby!"

I'm not going to yell *Hey* again, so I do a kind of formal salute and turn back toward the school. I actually would like to talk with her, but not right now, not like this. It's always been far-fetched that someone like me would become friends with someone like Izzy, but if it *were* to happen it would only be in the pure crucible of typing class where there would be no outside contaminants, such as her Neo-Thrasher colleagues.

"Kirby, come over here a sec!"

"I've got school," I call out.

"Don't be scared."

With that phrase, my fate is sealed. I have no choice but to comply.

Cromley

Once I get to the clearing, the Neo-Thrashers are situated in casual poses on the tables. I get the feeling I'm standing in a courtroom awaiting the verdict of a very laid-back tribunal. I take in a good whiff of the lingering smoke and I'll be damned if it doesn't actually smell like burning shoe rubber. Could that possibly be what they're smoking?

"Hey, Kirby," Izzy says. She's wearing a black pullover hoodie.

"That's the third time you've said, 'Hey, Kirby,'" I point out to her.

"Oh, yeah," she says with a giggle, "I guess I lost count." The others laugh along in a narcotized way.

"Well, it was good to see you," I say, "I'll be—"

"Friends, this here is Kirby Russo from my typing class. Kirby Russo, these are my friends from..." She pauses ditzily and then lets out a viscous laugh, "...shit... from wherever."

"Hi, dudes," I say.

None of them respond, so I turn to Izzy. "I better get going."

"You just got here."

"I have a hard enough time in my classes without being high on shoe rubber." Then I turn back to her friends. "Gentlemen, ladies, I'll leave you to your brain cell genocide."

As I start to walk away I hear snickering charged with a current of hostility. I hunch my shoulders, bracing myself in case one of the Neo-Thrashers decides to lob something at my back. I almost jump out of my shoes when the words, "Hey, wait up," buzz in my ear.

"You didn't have to be rude," Izzy says, falling into stride with me. "Those are my friends."

"I've got a lot going on right now, Izzy."

"Like what?" she asks. Her voice has returned to normal and I wonder if the stoned-out tone she'd had back there was part of an act.

Desperate and willing to take the risk, I tell her about the creepy guy in front of my house the other day. I tell her everything, down to the last detail, because it feels good to finally unburden the secret to someone, and because I haven't had much success decoding it on my own.

She's quiet for a while, staring straight ahead, hands fidgeting in the pockets of her pullover.

"Do you think this guy might be the reason Bradley's not coming back?" I ask.

She scrunches her mouth to one side for a second. "Did Bradley have any bad habits?" she asks. "Drugs? Gambling?"

"He's not really the habit type."

"I don't know," she says. "Sounds like it was more than just a social call."

"Seeing that guy made me miss Bradley again. Reminded me he's out there, you know?"

"Of course," she says gently. "It's so unresolved." We take a few steps together, feet touching the ground in unison. "This new guy, Harley, he's pretty bad?"

"He's different."

"Different's not necessarily bad, Kirby."

"No, but it's scary."

We take a few steps in silence. "Tell you what," she says. "Let me think on this creepy visitor situation. Get my head wrapped around it before I give you my analysis."

I steal a glance, catching her face in profile. Her bangs are a little longer than usual, nearly reaching her eyelashes. From the side, her nose is more aquiline than I'd realized. Her cheekbones are high, almost Indian-looking. I have to admit she's started to make a few mental cameos during my sessions with *The Art of Nude Photography.*

"You should be a model," I blurt.

"Shut up, Kirby." She pulls her hood over her head.

"I'm serious," I say, but it doesn't look like she believes me.

"Have you finished *Hamlet* yet?" she asks.

Cromley

"I've made some headway. But it's slow going."

She doesn't say anything, and it feels like a rebuke. We've entered the student parking lot now, and I slow my pace to prolong this time with her.

"I got in trouble with my mom for spending too much time on *Hamlet* and not on my schoolwork."

"She's probably nervous it's going to give you ideas."

"The weird thing is Uncle Harley thinks it's a good idea to read it. And he actually knows what it's about."

"How far have you gotten?"

"The part where he stabs Polonius," I say. "Don't tell me how it ends."

We've reached the side doors to the school and Izzy stops. An impish smile creeps onto her face.

"You want to see something cool?" She looks around to make sure the students shuffling past us aren't paying attention, which they're not.

She peels back the sleeve of her sweatshirt to expose the underside of her forearm. It's a surprisingly intimate act that leaves me lightheaded.

At first, it looks like a crusty scab on her skin. Then I notice a bluish shape underneath.

"What is it?"

"A tattoo," she says, beaming. "It's Mr. Yuk. You know, from those poison control stickers."

"Is it real?"

"Homemade. My friend Bodhi did it with a piece of guitar string and the ink from a ballpoint pen."

"Isn't that a good way to get AIDS?"

Her smile vanishes. "That's a shitty thing to say, Kirby." Her face is hard now, all sharp angles.

"It's just so...permanent."

"You sound like my mother," she snaps.

The Last Good Halloween

"I hate to say it, but your mother's probably right on this one."

"I thought you'd be way cooler about this," she says, easing her sleeve back down to her wrist. "Big mistake."

"I'm sorry," I say, sensing that more is at stake than I'd first realized. "Why'd you get Mr. Yuk? Why not get a dolphin jumping over a rainbow or something?"

She touches her arm lightly and winces. "I thought it looked tough."

"You already seem pretty tough to me," I say, but the words don't seem to register.

She nods and drifts back a step. The first period warning bell rings inside the school.

"So I'll see you in typing in a couple hours," I say optimistically.

"Sure," she says, but her eyes seem to say something else.

I pay zero attention in first period algebra and second period history. Instead I try to make as much headway as I can in *Hamlet*. The idea is to get a lot further in the play and then show Izzy about how far I've gotten. Maybe that'll help repair the breach from this morning.

When the bell rings for typing class, though, she isn't there. She doesn't come to class that day. And she doesn't come for the rest of the week.

Chapter 5

Now that I've finished *Hamlet*, I get why Izzy recommended it, but I don't see how it's supposed to help. The problem is that Hamlet seems to have a genuine affection for his dead father. And while I got along fine with Bradley, we were never close in a real father-son kind of way.

One of the few things we had in common was magic. This was early on. He and Debbie had been married less than a year. Once a week he'd come home from work and show me a new card trick. He'd do it a couple times at normal speed, and then once really slowly. After that he'd watch me as I tried to replicate it, over and over. He'd stand back with his index finger nestled contemplatively in the cleft of his chin. Occasionally he'd give me pointers. "Not like that," he'd say. "Flatten your thumb here to cover what your ring finger's doing underneath."

My hands were way too small at the time to do much convincing close-up work, but it didn't stop Bradley from trying. And I was so thrilled to have him take an interest in me that I faked liking magic for far longer than I actually liked it.

One of the high points of Bradley-as-father-figure came a year and a half after he'd moved in. There was a CPA conference in Spokane and, it just so happened, Doug Henning was scheduled to give a performance there that same weekend. Debbie wasn't thrilled about me going – after all, I was only ten and it would be my first time on an airplane – but I think she was really hoping it would launch our relationship on a good trajectory.

The first day, while Bradley had meetings, I hung out in our room watching TV, which was fine by me, since the hotel had a lot more channels than we did back in Billings.

That night, the night Doug Henning was to perform at the Spokane Civic Center, Bradley came back to the room, glanced around for a few seconds, and claimed to not be able to find the tickets. He asked me if I'd done something with them. Then he looked through his suitcase, taking the clothes out piece by piece, shaking and then refolding them on the bed. When this thorough search failed to turn up the tickets, he got some bottles from the mini-bar and began drinking.

Though my interest in magic had been waning for some time, I was still excited to see a true master of the art form. And now, at the last possible moment, the opportunity had been snatched away. I lay on the bed with my arms crossed, watching TV with the volume conspicuously high. Bradley sank into a deep funk. He sat there on his bed, motionless, except to drink from and refill his plastic hotel cup. It was a side of him I'd never seen before.

The show was supposed to start at 7:30, and as the time came and went, neither of us said a word. He was silently accusing me of losing the tickets, and I was simultaneously silently accusing him of never having them in the first place. Finally, around ten o'clock, he stood up so fast he knocked a couple mini-bottles onto the floor.

"I came here to see Doug Henning," he announced. "And I'm sure as hell gonna see Doug Henning!" He was agitated, so I knew better than to cross him. Bradley wore a trench coat that hung down past his knees. He had a gray scarf tucked in his pocket and one end dangled out and dragged in the slush.

Cromley

By the time we got to the Spokane Civic Center, the show was long over. No one was even lingering out front anymore.

"Hold on a sec." He walked down the block and peered into an alleyway. Then he waved me over. He pointed at a white limousine idling next to a set of nondescript emergency doors.

It took about twenty minutes of standing around, stamping our feet to keep warm, before Doug Henning finally emerged from the auditorium.

"Hey, Doug!" Bradley called.

The man did not stop or look over, just kept heading for the limousine, the door of which was being held open by a chauffeur.

"Mr. Henning, this kid here's one of your biggest fans."

Bradley must have correctly surmised that the words *kid* and *biggest* and *fan* would be enough to slow down even the most jaded of celebrities.

"He is, is he?" Doug had on a white parka with a fur-lined hood that made his head seem tiny.

"He's pretty good with the cards, Doug. You better watch your back when he gets older."

"My goodness," he said, playing along. "I'd better give him an autograph so he shows a little mercy on me." He reached into his pocket and pulled out a Magic Marker.

Bradley looked surprised at first and patted his own pockets. Then his face lit up. He took out his wallet and extracted a dollar bill. Doug shrugged, asked me my name and if I'd enjoyed the show. I said it was great.

He gave me the bill and climbed into his limousine. The dollar read: "Dear Kirby— Wishing you magical joy! —Doug Henning."

"That there is a good man," Bradley said with a sense of wonder in his voice. "A damn good man."

The exhaust of the limo dissipated. We, on the other hand, didn't have anywhere else to go. When we finally cabbed it back to the hotel room, Bradley said he was too keyed up for bed and wanted to grab a drink at the bar downstairs. I fell asleep and don't remember what time he got back.

The next evening we flew home to Billings. A couple weeks later, I told Bradley I wasn't interested in magic anymore. He was right in the middle of showing me a Rising Spades trick. He nodded and stopped the demonstration. We never talked about magic again. But to this day I carry that dollar bill with me like a talisman in my wallet, right behind my learner's permit.

As this event is one of the clearest, most vivid, memories I have of Bradley, I've lately been trying to dissect it for meaning. The truth is, I'm not entirely certain what it tells you about him as a father. I guess if I had to wrap it up and tie a ribbon around it, I'd say it means he wasn't fully equipped for fatherhood, though he did give it a solid try.

And if you wanted to go a little deeper and ask what the whole thing says about me as a son, I'd hem and haw for a while, then I'd eventually tell you I probably didn't make it very easy for him to be a dad.

The larger point I'm driving at here is that Hamlet actually admired and maybe even *loved* his father. While with me and Bradley, the strongest thing I could say is that I *appreciated* him. Still, I do think that's an underrated and important component of any healthy parental relationship. Appreciation is what I was used to. It's what I was comfortable with. And then, just like in the soap operas when they replace one actor with another and don't expect you to notice the difference, I'm supposed to switch my allegiances to Uncle Harley without asking a question.

I'm home from school and pleased to find no one else here. For the past week Debbie's been getting off work early and I've found her already cooking dinner or surrounded by stacks of folded laundry. One time, I came in and she was sitting in front of the TV, watching some infomercial about a revolutionary new fishing lure that wiggled under its own power. She had a blanket draped over her shoulders and I could see she'd been crying. When I asked her what the matter was, she said, "Those poor fish. They don't stand a chance." Until then, I'd had no idea Debbie was the slightest bit interested in animal rights.

The point is, I'm the type of guy who likes a little peace and quiet when he gets home. Usually, I'll rub one out in my bedroom, mix myself a cocktail, microwave a batch of egg rolls, then watch TV 'til someone gets back. It's my *me*-time. And I've been getting damn little of it lately. So it's no joke to say I'm seriously looking forward to some today.

I still use *The Art of Nude Photography*, but lately, it's more just a jumping off point for fantasies of Izzy. It's gotten so I have this fairly elaborate mental scenario where I catch her reclining on a wooden bench where she'd just been innocently daydreaming. She's not wearing a stitch of clothing except for a light blue ribbon in her hair. What I like about my scenario is that she's not too big in the breast department, which I think could be intimidating. If I made them too big in my head, it might suddenly turn me off because I don't know how I'd deal with a terribly big bosom in real life. I mean, seriously, what are you supposed to do with those things?

At first, Izzy's a little embarrassed when I walk by and notice her. Then I say something charming and funny that makes her laugh in a way where she throws her head back and then I kiss her neck, which she likes, obviously, since this is my fantasy, so why wouldn't she like it?

Anyway, the house is empty and I'm preoccupied with the mental task of constructing this scene when I happen to notice that the mail is undisturbed in the slot. Freshly arrived mail is one of the most unsanitized glimpses a kid can get into the adult world. So much of what's plopped into a mailbox hints at all the things we don't know or understand: bank statements; credit card bills; mortgage updates; insurance claims; magazines wrapped in black plastic. It's a treat every chance I get to look through it before anyone else.

At first, nothing jumps out. Gas and electric bills, both of which come in unsee-throughable envelopes and as such are useless to me; a J.C. Penney's catalog which is the height of tame – even the underwear section is lame, unless you're desperate, which I'm not. But then I come across a cream-colored, hand-lettered envelope, addressed to Debbie Russo. The writing is unmistakable – heavy, blue ballpoint, all caps. It belongs to none other than my erstwhile stepfather.

The Bradley-Returns Index suddenly has new life.

Mr. T lets out a pleading whine and spins in a tight circle at my feet. I can't tell if he's excited about the letter or if he just needs to pee.

"You know who this is from?" I ask him. "The once and possibly future head of this household. What do you think of that?"

Mr. T spins again, his nails clicking on the linoleum like a tap dancer. He fixes his glassy eyes on me and lets out an impatient growl. I let him out the back door to take care of his needs.

With shaky fingers, I hold the envelope up to the fading sunlight. No matter how long or hard I stare, it's too thick to make out any of its contents. It's such a tease to have possibly vital clues be so close yet so unobtainable.

I set off for the kitchen, fill up Debbie's kettle and set the gas on high. With nothing to do but wait, I pace back and forth across the linoleum, occasionally watching out the back window as Mr. T tries to pinpoint the optimal spot to make a deposit – hopefully right in the middle of Uncle Harley's organic vegetable garden.

I've never opened someone else's mail before, I swear. It's just that by reading this letter, I might get a better grasp of what to expect. Whether to prepare for Bradley's triumphant return, or to make my peace and usher in the Uncle Harley era with as much dignity as I can muster. After all, I'm a member of this family too.

Cromley

And I'm just as affected by all this uncertainty as everyone else. If you look at it the right way, I have an *obligation* to read it.

The kettle whistle blows and I hold the envelope flap up to it. A blast of steam hits my finger and I almost drop the letter onto the burner flames. Once I've got a safer angle established, I let the steam really soak into the seal, and slowly, with a little prying, the flap peels open. My fingers are starting to shake and my breathing's short and shallow.

Before going any further, I run to the front window to make sure no cars are pulling into the driveway. Then I go back to the kitchen and delicately extract the contents of the envelope. I'm half-convinced I should be wearing gloves, as if Debbie made a habit of dusting her mail for fingerprints.

The letter is written on nondescript cream-colored stationery.

> *My Love (yes, I'm using that word, and reserve the right to do so again in the future),*
>
> *I'm still "on the road," as you say, but I wanted to respond to some of the things you wrote in your last letter. So often fear makes us keep from each other the very things we most need to share. We bury these things deep within us and hope time will make them irrelevant. My love, I refuse to live my life like that and I refuse to let you do that either. That's why I told you those things the last time we spoke. It was never my intention to hurt you.*
>
> *As for your request: I feel as though I've failed you when I think about your asking me for a divorce. Maybe I'm being naïve, but I can't bring myself to say that's the answer. Marriages have been built on frailer ground than ours.*
>
> *The fact is, I still have a lot to sort out, feelings and emotions that need to see the purifying light of day. Only then will both of us be able to make the right decisions. Please know that this*

The Last Good Halloween

*letter is my lame way of saying I still love you and love who
you are.*

Yours,

Bradley

Two immediate sensations upon reading it: One, confusion.
There's a lot going on here that I'm not equipped to understand.
And two, disappointment that I didn't get a single mention in the
entire thing – not even a *P.S. Say hi to Kirby*, which has me a little
peeved.

And then a third sensation: a smoky burning smell. The
envelope's on fire!

I snatch it from the burner and flap out the flames. Which
unleashes a blizzard of black ash that floats around our kitchen like
a snow globe. A second later the smoke alarm starts to emit an ear-
splitting scream. Within a matter of seconds, this routine
reconnaissance mission has become FUBAR.

Knowing I have only minutes before Debbie gets home, I fly
into action. I throw open all the windows and doors to draw the
smoke out. Then I wet a big wad of paper towels and push it around
the linoleum to collect as many ashes as possible. By the time I'm
throwing it into the garbage bin, the air has cleared out enough that
the smoke alarm stops blaring. Even still, the room reeks of burnt
paper, and Debbie's got a world-class sniffer.

So I go to the freezer and retrieve a package of egg rolls. I dump
them on a plate and deposit them in the microwave, which I then
set for eight minutes, which should be sufficient to nuke those
suckers into oblivion.

While that element of my cover-up is gestating, the next
question is what to do about the letter. The envelope is half
destroyed; the side with the return address is gone, but the middle
part, with our address, is still visible. On its face this would seem to
be a deal-breaker, yet it's entirely possible Bradley would send a

letter with no return address, especially if he's on the move. So I run to the desk in the dining room and get a fresh envelope. Holding it over Bradley's original, I trace the old address onto the new one, being careful to preserve the integrity of Bradley's script.

When I'm done, I stuff the letter into the new envelope and reseal it. As the first few whiffs of burnt egg rolls begin wafting from the microwave, I can hear Debbie's Subaru sputtering into the driveway. Seconds left now, my heart is jack-hammering in my chest. I race back to the uncollected mail and, just as I'm sliding the letter into the middle of the stack, I realize my new envelope has neither a stamp nor a postmark, which, if Debbie notices – and she *will* – will make her think Bradley hand-delivered it, which could change the entire complexion of this situation in ways I can't possibly predict.

The smoke detector in the kitchen starts screaming again, this time from burnt Chinese food. I glance out the window. Debbie's coming up the front walk, purse tucked under her arm, car keys dangling from her index finger. She's probably seen me, so a mad dash for my bedroom will look suspicious. Out of options, I stuff the letter down my pants. Then I compose my face in the manner of a child who's accidentally overcooked some egg rolls but otherwise done nothing wrong.

Chapter 6

I'll concede that keeping Bradley's letter from Debbie may not have been the best thing in terms of repairing their fractured marriage, though at least this way I've got more time to really pore over it and unlock the hidden meaning. So far, I've scratched out a list of key elements that bear closer scrutiny.

1.   *My love*: I've never heard Bradley use that term of endearment (only the ambiguous *Pumpkin*) with my mother. It strikes me as both earnest and passionate – maybe even defiant – so I'll take that as a positive influence on the BRI.

2.   *the things we most need to share*: He says we bury them and hope they become irrelevant, which indicates that they must be pretty bad. The obvious assumption would be that Bradley was unfaithful. And yet, that's so out of keeping with his bookish and boring nature. I somehow doubt it. Either way, these "things" are the pivotal element of the letter, and determining what they are and neutralizing them will be crucial if the BRI is going to remain above zero.

3.   *feelings and emotions that need to see the purifying light of day*: Sounds like he regrets something and is engaged in serious soul searching. This also points toward infidelity, although he doesn't say "actions," so maybe we're talking

about something more mental than physical – a key distinction which makes me take that element, counter-intuitively perhaps, as a good sign.

4. *the divorce passage*: Debbie's given up and Bradley hasn't. Fairly cut-and-dried at first blush, but it's entirely conceivable that Debbie "gave up" as a defensive measure. Perhaps sensing the impending crash of her marriage, she decided to bail out first. And possibly, secretly, she's hoping her request for a divorce will be the thing that convinces Bradley to buck up, grab the controls, and bring this thing in for a smooth landing.

All in all, my assessment is that, yes, there are problems. But there's a lot to be optimistic about too. And with the right nudges, someone (possibly me) could intervene in a way that might still bring about a marital renaissance.

Frankly, the most disturbing thing about this letter is *not* the sad and sordid state of affairs between these two individuals. No, what's truly bothersome is that all this has been going on right in my own goddamned house without me having the slightest clue. When you're a kid, you have the luxury of recusing yourself from the concerns of the adult world. But when you do that, don't be surprised if you get back from computer camp to find out a shitstorm has done a number on everything you took for granted and didn't know you held dear.

I took a fresh look at what remains of the original envelope Bradley's letter came in. While the return address is toast, it does still have the postmark, which says the letter originated from Great Falls. He's got an older sister there, who we visited once a couple years ago on the way to Glacier National Park. As I recall, she had several pet ferrets and her house smelled of cedar chips and musky urine. She kept offering me cookies that she claimed she'd just baked, but later on I noticed the packages for them in her wastebasket.

Cromley

It's a pretty safe deduction that's where Bradley's holed up while he exposes his feelings and emotions to the purifying light of day. And just knowing this, I feel like I've gained a little control over the situation.

Debbie is standing at the kitchen sink, scrubbing the big skillet she cooked tonight's dinner in. She's wearing a Nitty Gritty Dirt Band t-shirt and faded jeans that taper at the ankles. Despite heavy ventilation, the rancid smell of blackened egg rolls is still detectable in the air. I'm standing just outside the kitchen doorway.

She's looking out the window, lost in thought as her hand scours circles against the worn-out Teflon. During the Bradley years, Debbie seemed to embrace her oncoming maturity. Sensible mom-like haircut, makeup that wasn't drawing too much attention to itself. Now she's letting her dishwater-blond curls hang down past her shoulders, and her makeup is straying toward the racy side of the color palette.

Tonight, she seems trapped in a deep reverie as she stares out into our backyard where the skeleton of my old swing set is slowly rusting away. The sky is turning from slate gray to chalkboard black.

It used to be easy to read Debbie. These days, it's as if there's always a second emotion hiding just under the surface. She's more up and down, unpredictable. Which definitely supports my thesis that Bradley, while not a dazzling persona, did provide this family with some much-needed and well-appreciated (by me at least) stability.

"Why are you staring at me?" she asks. Now that it's dark out, my reflection has become visible in the windowpane.

"I'm not."

She flips the sink on to rinse the skillet. "Okay, then what were you just thinking while you were standing there *not* staring at me?"

"It's funny," I say. "I was just wondering the exact same thing about you."

The Last Good Halloween

She sets the skillet in the rack and turns to face me.

"I swear, Kirby, sometimes it's like pulling teeth to have a conversation with you."

"Sometimes a conversation with you is like having teeth pulled."

She pats her forehead with the back of her hand. "I did not abuse you enough as a child," she says.

Then she smiles and eventually starts to laugh. It's a nice sparkling laugh that sounds like something that feels pretty good.

"Have you finished your homework?"

I nod noncommittally and ask, "Have you heard from Bradley lately?"

She shakes her head.

"Aren't you worried about him? I know I sure am."

She wrings the sponge out and sets it next to the faucet. "Did you ever consider that the man might not want to come back?"

"I don't think so. I think something's stopping him."

A look of what might be nervousness crosses her face. "What makes you say that?" she asks.

If she thinks I'm going to spill what I know about the creepy visitor and the letter, she's crazier than I thought. Those two pieces of information are my only leverage.

"It's just a hunch, Debbie."

She looks down at the checkerboard on the linoleum a moment as if she were trying to count something in its pattern. "Have you ever seen one of those insects caught in amber?" she asks. "The ones they sell at souvenir shops."

"I think so."

"You know how that happens? It's just some prehistoric tree sap that the bug accidentally stepped into and got caught. And it struggled to get out but couldn't. Until it got completely covered, stuck for eternity."

Cromley

This is exactly what I'm talking about with the secondary emotions lurking in the background. I have no idea what she's really thinking right now.

"Mom, what's your point?"

"My point is, did you ever wonder what it must be like for that bug when the sap covered it over?"

"I hadn't thought about it," I say.

She slides her hands into her pockets, elbows tucked in close at her sides. "You know, Kirby, the one thing I've always done is provide. I never depended on a man to take care of us. I promised myself I'd never put us in a situation where we had no options."

"Does that mean Uncle Harley is optional?"

"Optional for me. Not you." She smiles. And if I were standing closer to her I think she'd ruffle my hair.

"I know this is a tough adjustment," she says. "Don't think that hasn't occurred to me."

"I'm just worried. I don't see any kind of long term plan here, Debbie."

"You gotta trust that your mom is doing the best she can, for both of us. We're in this together – we always will be."

I now see she's angling for a sentimental, you-and-me-against-the-world moment here. Part of me would love to play along, but her defenses are down and I'd be remiss if I didn't take this opportunity to acquire some intel.

"So I came across something interesting in the mail last week."

Her left eyelid flickers just slightly, as if a tiny drop of lemon juice had been errantly squeezed. Then she leans against the counter and folds her arms across her chest, back in control after a momentary slip. I don't know what I was hoping for here, and I don't know what this reaction tells me beyond what I already knew or guessed.

"What was that?" she asks.

The Last Good Halloween

My mind scrambles for a second. "I was looking through the J.C. Penney catalog and thinking maybe I should switch from wearing briefs to boxers."

"Why is that, do you think?" She cocks her hips to the side. Now that she's weathered my initial salvo, nothing's going to faze her.

"I think maybe boxers are more mature. People at school call briefs tighty-whiteys. They're kind of for kids."

Debbie takes this in with a slow nod. "Yes," she says, "but studies have shown that boxers raise the male sperm count. The last thing I want is to increase my teenage son's fertility rate."

Now it's Debbie's turn to watch and observe, so I try to minimize the fidgeting I would normally do when my mother talks about this kind of stuff in front of me. Whatever reaction she was hoping for, she seems to have gotten it, because she eventually smiles and says, "Maybe we'll get you one pair. Add them to your underwear cycle. If they're a hit, we'll switch you over."

She uncrosses her arms and pushes herself away from the sink.

"Shake on it," she says.

Her skin is still warm and soft – almost fragile – from the dishwater. And I realize for the first time that my hand is larger than hers.

Julian and I eat lunch and walk home together almost every day now. Like so many undocumented rituals of high school, ours has taken shape without any real discussion. It's just kind of happened that way, and neither of us has the energy to disrupt the status quo. This afternoon we're almost through Prospect Park when Julian asks:

"Have you heard anything from your stepdad?"

I'm a little surprised by the question. I haven't told him about the creepy visitor or Bradley's letter, mostly because I think he'd be more clueless on the relationship nuances than me. The person I really want to talk with is Izzy, but she hasn't been to school in a week.

"Nothing new," I say.

Julian's found a plastic Dr. Pepper bottle which he's kicking along as we walk. "A while ago, you asked what it was like to have a real family."

"That sounds possible," I say.

He toes the pop bottle and it cartwheels end over end. He seems deeply absorbed in its progress. "I guess I'm curious what it's like to not have a real family."

"I don't follow."

"Do you remember what it was like when your mom got divorced from your father?"

"Debbie was never married to the Original Biological Contributor. And he was gone long before I could remember anything. My gut instinct would be to say it's been easier that way, but it's not as if my life's been a creamy bowl of oatmeal."

Julian swipes his foot at the bottle. It shanks off his heel and skitters into the gutter.

"And then with Bradley not coming home, that all happened when I was at computer camp. So it seems like these things tend to happen when I'm not around. I'm not saying I'm the one holding everything together. I just think the adults usually try to handle all that stuff out of sight of the kids."

Julian mumbles something and sinks his hands into his pockets.

"Are things bad at home?" I ask cautiously, in case this is an overreach.

"Things are fine," he says, but he makes the mistake of looking at me and I can see his eyes are red-rimmed; his lips are nearly bruised purple from his biting at them.

We're at the southeast corner of the park now. Time for me to split off north toward home. But something's telling me Julian's not ready to face whatever's waiting for him at his.

The Last Good Halloween

"I am kind of an expert on these things," I say. "If you want, I can help." The offer is beyond the scope of our friendship as it currently stands, and part of me regrets extending it.

Julian's quiet for a moment. He looks down the street toward his house then back at me. He nods slightly.

"First," I say, "let's run through a Marital Distress Checklist." I retrieve the guttered Dr. Pepper bottle and kick it back to him. "Okay, number one: Do they still sleep in the same bedroom?"

"Yes," he says confidently. "I mean sometimes one'll sleep on the couch, but not usually." He kicks the bottle to me. "Is that bad?"

"Inconclusive. Number two: Do you ever see evidence of PDAs?"

Julian gives me a quizzical look.

"Public displays of affection. Do they kiss or hold hands or anything where you can see it?"

"No," he says, "but they never did that before either."

"Okay. Number three: Work hours. Have they increased lately?"

Julian thinks about this a minute. "My dad has been spending more time at the office. So, yeah, I guess so."

"All right. Last question: Fights? Talk about that."

I kick the bottle back to him and he traps it with the heel of his Top-Sider.

"Lots," he says. "Twice a week. Maybe more. Then they won't talk to each other for like a day afterwards. Sometimes it's like they only talk to each other in order to fight."

"What are they fighting about?"

"Pretty much anything," he says. "But lately I think it's because they're trying to have another kid and they're not really able to."

"Another kid? At their age? That's not a good sign, buddy."

"Yeah, that's what I thought." His voice has dropped so that now it's barely a whisper. He doesn't need any more analysis from me to know his parents' marriage is tanking. He's heard his own answers.

"I know it's hard," I tell him. "Admitting all this stuff."

Cromley

He's still got his heel on the bottle. He rolls it under his foot slowly, the plastic sides crunching.

"Sometimes I just wish I could get away from them," he says.

"You've got a few more years before that can happen. Right now, the best thing you can do is become as self-sufficient as possible. It's going to come in handy down the road."

"What do you mean, self-sufficient?"

"Basically, you—"

A car horn lets out a three-note trill behind me. When I turn around, I see the Millers' Vanagon swerve over to the shoulder and come to a stop. Mrs. Miller leans over and looks across the park at us. Julian sees her and freezes.

Mrs. Miller hits the horn again – three short, one long, which leaves me wondering if that's Morse code for anything.

"Your mom," I say, because so far he hasn't shown the faintest hint of recognition.

One long, sustained horn blast.

"Sounds like she's in a hurry."

"Uh-huh." His gaze is unfocused, vacant. He's not going anywhere on his own.

"Why don't I walk you to the car?"

I give a wave to let Mrs. Miller know that we're on the way and she can take it easy with the goddamned horn. I grab Julian by the elbow and steer him toward the street. He lifts his foot off the Dr. Pepper bottle and shuffles along with me.

Mrs. Miller is alone in the car, yet Julian inexplicably slides open the rear door and sits in back. She unrolls the window and leans across the passenger seat. Her red hair hangs past her shoulder and dangles as she sways a little unsteadily.

"Hi, Kirby." Her voice is rich and warm, as if she'd just finished telling a joke I wasn't privy to.

"Hi, Mrs. Miller. You're looking well." This is actually not true. Her skin is a sickly greenish hue.

The Last Good Halloween

"It's really good to see you, Kirby." Again, there's that overly solicitous tone in her voice that feels like a joke I'm not getting. She blinks and her lids seem so heavy it's a struggle to open them back up.

"Thank you." I'm a half-second from turning and getting the hell away from her.

"I know you must be having a hard time adjusting," she says.

"Adjusting to what?" I shoot a glance back at Julian. He's facing forward, oblivious as a crash test dummy.

"It's important to know that God doesn't put any test in front of us that he thinks we can't pass."

I'd love to point out that the algebra test God put in front of me last week was completely unpassable. But my urge to be a smartass is trumped by a need to know what she's getting at. So instead, I go with:

"What test do you think God's putting in front of me, Mrs. Miller?"

"Oh," she says, "I didn't mean to—"

"Mom, can we go home now?" Julian blares from the backseat.

She sits up and tucks her hair behind an ear. "I just want you to know, Kirby, that I'm organizing a prayer tree at church for your mother. And for your stepfather."

The skin on my arms goes goose-bumpy. "What do you know about—"

"I know it's difficult," she says, leaning back behind the wheel. "Just remember, it's never too late for any of us to turn to face the Lord."

She pops the van into drive and pulls out from the curb. But she failed to check her blind spot because she nearly sideswipes a Camaro, which just manages to swerve out of her way. I catch a Doppler-blurred "Fuck you, lady," as the car carries on, and the Vanagon, a little more cautiously now, merges into the traffic.

Chapter 7

Just when it seems like I'll have to slog through typing as friendlessly as all my other classes, I show up one morning to find Izzy sitting there, back straight, fingers poised over the keys like a sprinter who's just been called to her mark. It's still a few minutes before the bell and Mr. Gorton hasn't come in yet.

"Where were we?" she asks out of the corner of her mouth.

I'm not sure if *we* refers to her-and-me or to the class in general, so I slide behind my typewriter and say, "I thought you'd abandoned me."

"I considered it." She's wearing more makeup than usual – a thick underscore of eyeliner and some kind of nearly black lipstick that makes her face look like paraffin.

"Where've you been?"

"Working," she says. "Extra shifts." Her fingernails are bitten down to the quick and painted a color that matches her lipstick. She's wearing a T-shirt that says, *Do I Dare Disturb the Universe?* "Too tired to drag my ass in here."

"You have a job?" I ask, before managing to catch myself. It's these kinds of questions that betray my naiveté, make me seem younger than I really am.

"Of course, numb-nut."

The Last Good Halloween

She closes her eyes for a moment, then slowly reopens them as if she expects to find herself somewhere else.

"Where do you work?"

"I'm a waitress," she says.

"Where?" The thought that Izzy has a whole other side of her life that could be so unknown to me has me feeling a little uneasy.

"Nowhere." She does the eye-close thing again.

"Come on. Where do you waitress?"

"Kirby, please."

"Are you afraid I'll show up and hassle you and leave a lousy tip?"

This manages to draw out a reluctant smile. "Trust me," she says, "you're not going to show up where I work."

She has no idea I'd be more than happy to press her all day on this question. But she lucks out when Mr. Gorton trudges into the room and announces we'll be taking a timed quiz on page 129.

Izzy switches her machine into word processing mode and taps out the first line. Today, when Mr. Gorton tells us to begin, he doesn't prowl the room looking for the culprit, although he does cast what seems like a longer-than-usual glance in our direction.

After running my results through the score calculating equation, I come up with a solid B. Typing is shaping up to be my strongest academic subject. We hand our papers forward and wait to hear our assignment for the day.

"How's the tattoo?" I whisper.

"It got a little infected, but it's better now." She turns her wrist to show me the underside of her arm. The image is a reasonable facsimile of the Dr. Yuk face, with squinted eyes, frowning mouth and tongue hanging down in disgust. Debbie used to put those stickers on all the bottles she kept under the kitchen sink.

"Do you regret doing it?" It's a dangerous question, given how our last tattoo conversation ended, but I want to show her I'm not afraid to talk about hard topics.

Cromley

She gives me a look out of the corner of her eye. "No," she says flatly. She's about to leave it at that, but then adds, "Maybe it isn't what I would have wanted or where. But regret implies that it actually matters. Which it doesn't."

Mr. Gorton looks up from the sheaf of quizzes he's fanning like a poker hand. "Okay, class," he says, "turn to page 176 and begin doing exercise number 4. I'll collect it at the end of the period."

After a while, I nudge Izzy and type:

`I finished Hamlet.`

She glances up at Mr. Gorton, who has a newspaper spread out flat on his desk. He's trying to make it look like he's entering stuff in his grade book, though it's pretty obvious he's doing the Jumble.

Izzy types: `And?`

I hadn't really thought of what to say about *Hamlet*, and while my brain scrambles for something intelligent to type, she adds: `Thoughts?`

I type: `It's kind of close to my situation.`

She types: `And?`

I type: `Vut Hamlet's fahter was dead. My stepdad is missing. Big difference.`

She types: `Is that all you came up with?`

I'm starting to wonder if she's paying me back for the questions I asked earlier.

I type: `Maybe it's just tha`

At that moment the papers in both our machines are simultaneously ripped clean out. It happens so fast that my next few key clacks strike the empty platen. And the ensuing shock is enough to make us both jump back in our chairs as we look up to see Mr. Gorton's scowling mug hovering overhead.

"Was there something wrong with the assignment I gave you?" he snarls.

"No, sir," Izzy says.

The Last Good Halloween

"Because this," he points at our typing, "is not the assignment I gave you."

"Actually," I say, "what we were working on was more difficult and possibly even has more real-world applicability."

Mr. Gorton pauses for a split second. "It's not the assignment I gave you," he says again.

"You're actually upset with us for trying to challenge ourselves academically? Incredible."

His face goes scowlier. "This is a conversation we're going to finish after school," he says, "when I see you both for detention."

Izzy nods, ready for this to be over. I, of course, am barely getting started.

"Detention? What is this, a Soviet gulag?" I can feel the wide sheep-eyes of every student in the classroom on me.

"That's enough, Mr. Russo." A hint of panic has crept into his voice and it's enough to lure me onward.

"You know, sir, the *true* crime here is your pedagogical technique."

Mr. Gorton blinks five times in rapid succession. Then he does something that catches everyone in the room off-guard. His massive Frankenstein hand shoots out and pincers me at the back of the neck, just below the base of the skull. His grip is viselike. The pain is so bad my eyes start to water and my fingertips go numb. The jowls under his chin quiver with suppressed rage.

"I've had all I can stand, Mr. Russo." His eyes are blue lasers, locked on mine, motionless.

"Mr. Gorton, we'll be here," Izzy says, pleading. Which I'm immeasurably grateful for because I can barely talk right now. "Please," she says, "we'll come for detention."

His grip loosens. I can feel my fingertips again.

The bell rings and Mr. Gorton finally lets go. He exhales and turns back to his desk. Reluctantly, the rest of the students begin peeling away. They've gotten their USRDA of conversational fodder. Izzy and I gather our things and make a hasty retreat.

"Why did you do that?" I ask once we've made it into the hallway.

"Hold on," she says, clutching her books to her chest. "You're mad at me?"

"I didn't need you to rescue me back there."

"Quit it, Kirby. You're being a psycho."

I freeze. Is it possible she knows about the Velcro shoes? "Why did you say that?"

"Say what? You're being a spaz."

"You called me a psycho."

"Psycho. Spaz. Whatever. Quit being one."

"Maybe *you're* being one."

She wheels on me, red faced. "You sound like a child," she says.

Her words cut right through me. My face goes hot.

"*I'm* being a child?" I sputter. "I'm not the one scrawling some stupid picture on my skin. I'm not the one smoking things I don't even know what they are."

"You think you *get* me, Kirby? You think you *know* me? You don't have a clue about the shit I have to go through every day."

She turns and leaves me there in the hallway. The space she vacated slowly fills in with students flowing from class to class.

This morning I lost one of two people in this school who I could reasonably call a friend. Now, it's lunch time and I'm about to jettison the other.

Julian's waiting at my locker when I get there.

"Hey," he says as I begin working the dial.

I don't give him so much as a glance of acknowledgement.

"Everything all right?" he tries.

The Last Good Halloween

I cram my books into my locker and slam the door closed. "I've got other lunch plans today, Julian."

His gaze drops and he curls his lower lip under his teeth. As I'm turning to leave, he asks, "Is it because of what my mom said?"

"It's because I can't trust you. For all I know you're the one who wrote this." I point to TIPSY-CHOICE on my locker door.

"I don't even know what that means," he says, holding his hands up.

"What did you tell your mom about Bradley?"

"Nothing. I swear to God."

"How could you betray me like that?"

He tries to grab my shoulder, but I shake him off.

"My mom finds out all kinds of stuff from her church friends. They're always gossiping on the phone. You've got to believe me."

"Sorry, Julian, you're on your own from here on out."

"Kirby, wait, don't go."

But he's already talking to my back, and a second later he's talking to the hallway.

Roosevelt's a big school, though it feels a lot smaller when you're trying to avoid someone. I hustle over to Kwik Way across the street and pick up some beef jerky and a Mr. Pibb. Eating in the cafeteria's out of the question, since that's where Julian'll be. So I end up in the auxiliary gym, which the P.E. classes only use when they're playing badminton. To stay out of sight, I find a spot behind the rolled-up wrestling mats. It's dusty and smells like ballsweat, but at least I'm alone and don't have to worry about being disturbed by anyone. Which is the way I've always preferred it.

Detention wasn't what I'd expected. Izzy and I showed up at the classroom, and Mr. Gorton gave us the original page 176 assignment. That was it. No mention of the neck-squeezing altercation. No angry rehashing of who was at fault. As we got to work, he sat at his desk and held the newspaper up like a screen, so all we could see were his fingertips curled around the edges of the sports section. When we finished, he collected our assignments and said he'd see us tomorrow. I was impressed with the way he was able to not hold our earlier encounter against me. It was as if we were two actors who'd played mortal enemies on stage, yet off stage we were just a couple of old hams.

Now Izzy and I are walking together through the student lot. I'm on my way home. I have no idea where she's going. As I glance at her, I realize that the curve on her nose is just a tiny bit crooked, not a natural aquiline; most probably the result of a long ago break that was set badly. She's not beautiful in the way most people would think a girl is hot. There's just something about her I like looking at.

I'm not really sure where we stand on the friendship-scale, after this morning's hallway blowup, so I decide to go with something generic: "I like your T-shirt. *Do I Dare Disturb the Universe?* That's catchy."

"It *should* be," she says without breaking stride. "It's from 'The Love Song of J. Alfred Prufrock.'"

There's a momentary pause wherein I must decide if I should pretend to know what she's talking about or not.

"By T.S. Eliot?" she says.

"Oh," I say.

"Come on, Kirby. You haven't read it?"

"You really have to stop doing that," I say.

"Doing what?" she asks, all innocent.

"You know what I mean. The constant literary references, then the complete surprise if I don't get it. Highly obnoxious."

"For the record," she says, "I only do that because it's fun to watch your reaction."

We reach the edge of the lot and enter the park. Izzy glances over at the picnic tables where her Neo-Thrasher friends often linger. They're empty.

"I've been thinking about *Hamlet*," I say.

She inclines her head to let me know she's listening.

"It's hard because you don't really know the back story. You don't have a feel for how strong Hamlet's relationship was with his dad before he died."

"Are you telling me *Hamlet* would be a better play if it had flashbacks?"

"Not a lot of them. Maybe just one childhood bonding scene so we could see how close they were. Something that tells you what he was like as a dad."

"Kirby," she says, "what does that have to do with anything?"

"I'm just saying things in my house are a little more complex."

She shakes her head.

"Here's the thing," I say. "Hamlet's father was definitely killed by Claudius. So it's easy to see why he did what he did in the end. But what if Bradley and Debbie are having marital issues, and the Uncle-Harley-moving-in part is just a symptom of those issues?"

Izzy looks down and studies her feet for a few steps. "Marital issues?"

It's a two-word question, but it's all the opening I need to tell her about Bradley's letter. I've studied the thing so closely by now I can practically recite it to her verbatim. I even tell her about how I burnt the envelope but managed to save the postmark. All of this comes pouring out of me so fast I don't have time to gauge her reaction.

"So," I say, "the mystery deepens."

She flexes her eyebrows. "It would seem so."

"What do you think Hamlet would do in my situation?"

"More importantly," she says, "what would Kirby do?"

It's quiet for a moment and I realize she's waiting for an answer.

"Don't think about it too much," she says. "The whole point of the play is to take action, right? To be or not to be? So what action will Kirby take? How will he *be*?"

Cromley

Hearing Izzy couch it in the blunt terms of Hamlet's binary sets loose a wave of adrenaline. My head swims for a second as we walk.

"Ever since I got the letter, I've been kicking an idea around," I admit.

She nods expectantly.

"I mean, it seems like maybe they could get back together if they just sat down and talked things out. You know?"

"I hear you," Izzy says, her enthusiasm growing.

"And maybe they're each worried about being the first one to admit they're wrong."

"Could be."

"So what if I tracked him down? What if I convinced Bradley to come back home?"

"You said he's staying in Great Falls, right?"

I nod. "With his sister."

"I think you already know the answer," she says. "You *have* to."

Then the last of the adrenaline washes out of my system, leaving me with a dry mouth and a realist's eye.

"At least it's nice to think about," I say.

"Thinking!" she says, incensed. "I thought we said no more thinking! Doing!"

"I don't have a car, Izzy. I don't even have a real license."

Her gaze lingers on the empty tennis courts for a moment.

"It's easy to come up with reasons to *not* do something bold," she says.

"It's easy because the reasons exist. I'm just a fucking kid."

"Listen," she says, "you yourself said Bradley might be in trouble. That guy in front of your house wasn't playing around. Don't you think you should do everything within your power to help him? Especially if that means getting him to come back?"

She's got a point. Neither of us says anything for a while.

The Last Good Halloween

We've come to the edge of the playground – a big circle of sand, dominated by a thick-timbered fort in the center. It's too cold out today for anyone to be playing on it. Izzy looks up at the abandoned equipment.

"We haven't known each other very long, have we, Kirby?"

"This morning you said I didn't know you at all."

"Heat of the moment," she says, shrugging it off. She pulls her hand out of her coat pocket and scatters a handful of lint. "You know what I like about you?"

"No."

"You've got the courage of your convictions."

I shake my head. "You lost me."

"Everyone around here has a *thing*. Some gimmick that helps them blend, helps them fit in. Everyone's a member of some pack. Me included." She smiles wistfully. "You don't do that."

"You're assuming I had a choice," I say. "I don't remember being asked."

Izzy takes her hand out of her pockets slowly. "Kirby, you are exactly who you are. And that's a rare thing."

I'm not really sure where this is coming from or what it's building toward. Although I like the sound of it, so I'm not going to ruin it by talking.

"A very rare thing," she says.

And then something happens that pretty much blasts me out of the water. As we're standing there, surveying the empty playground, Izzy grabs me by the elbow, turns me toward her, and plants one right on my lips. A kiss.

It happens so fast – all told, it's probably one second of motion – that I really don't have time to react. One instant I'm standing there, breathing in the cold air, and the next, I have a pair of lips pressed against mine. I'm aware of a smoky aura around her, which if I had more time to think I'd probably find unappealing, but since I don't, it's just a piece of unprocessed sensory data. Her lips are cold at first. Then they warm up and they're soft and alive in a way I can't really describe. I don't care how many times you plan for it, or try to imagine it, or even simulate it, there's nothing that can prepare you for the real thing.

Then, as quickly as it began, she pulls away and starts fast-walking back toward the school.

"Izzy!" I call out. "Where are you going?"

"Think about how you're going to be, Kirby." She waves her hand over her shoulder as she walks over the pale autumn grass.

"How can you leave after something like that?"

She keeps waving and walking, then stops waving and keeps walking 'til she's out of sight. And I have no choice but to wander – dazed, lightheaded, alone – home.

I'd like to believe what happened in the park somehow transcended carnality. It would be nice if I could say it was some pure expression of pristine something. But the fact is, by the time I get home, I'm feeling pretty goddamned horny, ready to bolt into my room and just have at it. I won't even need *The Art of Nude Photography* today. I've already concocted a new scenario where I happen to pass the playground at night and Izzy's in the top tower of the timber fort and she's calling me to go up there and I do and...you get the point.

As it turns out, detention set back my arrival time late enough that Debbie and Uncle Harley are both home when I get in, and there's basically no chance I'm going to get the kind of me-time I need right now.

In fact, dinner's almost ready, which is seemingly all fine and dandy. But instead of smelling dinner (chicken breasts, beet salad, wild rice), I should have smelled an ambush, because that's what it is. As soon as the three of us sit down, Debbie starts up with:

"I received a phone call today from your typing teacher."

From there it goes downhill rapidly. I'll spare you the grotesque details. The upshot is that while Uncle Harley gazes on with a practiced look of concern, Debbie goes for the histrionics. "Where did I go wrong?" and "What more do you want from me?"

As much as possible, I keep my answers to one word: "Nowhere" and "Nothing."

The whole time I keep thinking: This is it. Strike three. Good-bye, Roosevelt High. Hello, Haverford Military Institute.

As Debbie's words wash over me, I find myself feeling oddly relieved. I suppose this was always bound to happen. Though if I do have one regret it's that I would've preferred strike three to be something more memorable than mouthing off to the idiotic Mr. Gorton.

"The things you said, Kirby. To a teacher. I'm ashamed."

"Before you nominate him for sainthood, you should know he pinched the back of my neck. It was borderline abusive."

She closes her eyes and shakes her head. "I know perfectly well what he did. He told me everything. And I told him he can do that whenever he sees fit."

There's no point arguing.

"I just don't know anymore," she says. "I just don't know."

Here it comes – the final verdict: they'll probably make me wear a goony uniform at this new school and do pushups when I misbehave. Seeing the end before me, I decide to embrace it with a little style. I slap my hands on the table and bellow:

"Fuck this! I don't take shit from no one!"

There's a ringing silence in the dining room as Debbie and Uncle Harley exchange glances. Finally Debbie speaks,

"Oh great. Now he's using double negatives."

Classic Debbie, to be more worried about improper grammar than the possible slide of her only son into a life of outlaw degeneracy.

She works me over pretty good for another hour or so, then does something truly shocking. She sends me to my bedroom without mentioning strike three. It seems unlikely that this was an oversight, and I can only assume it means I've been granted clemency. Which I suppose should make me happy, but mostly just raises a lot of perplexing questions as to what my boundaries are.

I pace back and forth across the bedroom, too worked up to even try conjuring my new Izzy-Playground fantasy. Finally, when things have quieted down in the house, I slink out to the hallway phone and dial one of the few numbers I know by heart. I'm braced for the possibility that Mrs. Miller could answer, which'll necessitate some fancy explanation for why I happen to be calling so late. Fortunately, Julian picks up.

"What is it, Kirby?"

"I've decided to forgive you."

He absorbs this for a moment. I can hear a racket going on in the background. Sounds like a howling skirmish is in full session at Chez Miller tonight.

"Thanks," he says, "but it wasn't my fault. I didn't tell her anything."

"I'm not interested in assigning blame, Julian. The simple fact is you owe me."

"Owe you what?"

"I'm still in the planning stages," I whisper. "I'll let you know soon enough."

Chapter 8

When you're trying to negotiate with someone, it's best to remain as vague as possible for as long as possible. Get them to agree to an abstract principle before they know the precise idea. That's why I decide to lead off with:

"I need one day, Julian."

It's Thursday after school and we're walking along the south edge of the park. For strategic reasons, I've waited until this precise moment to make my pitch: the day I need is tomorrow.

"One day for what?" he asks.

I'm swallowing spit to make sure my throat stays moist and doesn't give off any telltale voice-cracking. You never want the negotiatee to know how nervous you are.

"The way I look at this thing, Julian, it's one day in your entire life."

"What *thing*?"

"You've been alive nearly 5,000 days, okay?"

He nods grimly, as if this is something he disagrees with yet doesn't have the facts to back him up.

"With a little luck, you probably have 23,000 days left. So realistically, all we're talking about is three one-hundred-thousandths of your life."

The Last Good Halloween

"What are you talking about?" He sounds irritated, a testament to how much my argument has already rattled him.

"I just wanted to give a little context for this discussion."

"Discussion of *what*?!"

We're getting near the corner of the park where we usually part ways, and I need to get him on the hook before that point or it'll be too easy for him to slip away.

"I have a problem, Julian, and you have the ability to help me."

"How?"

"As you know, my stepfather has left town. What I haven't told you is he's staying in Great Falls. And I have reason to believe that, with the proper motivation, he can be convinced to return and serve out his term as my father."

Julian burrows his hands into his coat pockets.

"In order to pull this off, I'll need your help. I need to cash in that favor you owe me."

"What am I supposed to do?" he asks.

I take it as a good sign that he doesn't question the validity of the favor-debt, which, if he did, would've added a whole extra layer to an already complex argument.

"You can help..." Short pause. Make him wait for it. "...by giving me one day."

He throws his hands up at his sides, frustrated by the circle I've just led him in. My position feels strong, so, like a matador, I go in for the kill.

"I need to borrow your dad's Roadrunner."

"What?"

"For one day."

He says *what* again, but this time it's barely a whisper and afterwards he gulps at the air as if these few breaths might be his last.

Cromley

"We'll take off early tomorrow morning. Great Falls is three hours away. There by noon. I find Bradley. Show him the error of his ways. Boom! Home by 3:30. No one'll even miss us."

"I don't think..." His voice trails off.

"We'll call in sick tomorrow morning so they won't be looking for us at school. Trust me, I've thought of everything."

"What if we get caught?"

"The plan is perfect." To prove my point, I take out a piece of notebook paper I've got folded up in my pocket and wave it in the air. It's actually more of a checklist than a plan, though I hardly expect him to note the distinction. I push on, "Nothing can go wrong with this plan, Julian."

"Why me?" he asks. "Why not just you go and leave me out of it?"

It's true. There's no obvious reason why he should participate. This is *my* thing, and, by rights, I should handle it on my own. There are two reasons I'm asking Julian to be a part of it. One – obviously and selfishly – is that I need his dad's car. Ever since The Event, Debbie guards her keys like they contain the nuclear launch codes. Secondly, and more altruistically, a road trip might do good things for Julian. As the rafters and joists of his family begin to fall apart, he's going to need to find a life outside that formerly sound structure. I wasn't kidding when I told him a while back that he needs to become self-sufficient. A trip like this might show him he's capable of more than he realizes.

"I'm asking you because you've never in your life done anything this much against the rules. When it's over and when we've pulled it off, it's something you'll remember forever. You'll tell your grandkids about it, and they'll be shocked by how cool a guy their grandfather is. Everything else you do will be measured against this one day."

Julian fiddles with the strap on his backpack for a moment. He seems to be deep in thought.

The Last Good Halloween

"That's what being young is about," I pile on. "That's what being *alive* is about. It's what myths are made of."

"Of course you need my dad's car, too," he says. "I mean, you couldn't do it without that."

"Truth be told, I'd rather not take your dad's car, Julian. Give me an invisible Taurus over a Roadrunner any day. But his is the only car I can think of that people wouldn't miss if we borrowed it for a day."

We've reached the edge of the park. Julian looks off across the street in the direction of his house. The trees nearby are bare and stark. Their leaves lie in scattered piles where the wind has left them.

I'm counting on two motivating forces to push Julian over the edge. The first is his parents' imminent divorce, which I've already alluded to. Couple that with the natural predisposition of most kids that come from hyper-Christian families to rebel against the strictures of their households, and you've got a pretty combustible psychic cocktail. Frankly, his parents'll be lucky if the worst thing he does in the coming years is borrow their car for a day.

"Can I ask you something?" Julian says.

I nod.

"I get why you think *I* should do this. That's actually straightforward. But I don't get why you'd want to do it."

"I didn't hear a question there, Julian."

"You *say* it's to get your stepfather to come home. But I don't think that's all of it."

"Okay," I say, a little surprised by his line of thinking. "What if I told you he might be in some trouble, and maybe he needs my help?"

He glances at his watch and bites his lip. "That may be true, but I don't think that's it either. What's the *real* reason you want to do this, Kirby?"

Cromley

Again, he catches me off-guard. I don't know if this is just a lucky guess on Julian's part, or if he's routinely capable of this kind of piercing insight. But I do know I'm going to have to reevaluate him as a person and friend when this is over.

"If I tell you why, does it mean you'll do it?"

He eyes me suspiciously. "It depends on your answer."

I refold my plan and slide it back into my pocket. We're off daylight savings time now and the sky is already sliding towards darkness. I've only got a few minutes left to close the deal. It's time for a radical strategy of complete honesty.

"The Primary Objective is to get him to come home. Plain and simple. But if he absolutely won't or can't come home, then my Secondary Objective is to find out why."

Julian nods once, a signal to keep going.

"I've lost plenty of father figures before Bradley came along, so this is nothing I'm not used to. But I really thought he was the one who'd stick." My throat squeezes closed momentarily and I have to cough to keep it open. "I mean, is there something wrong with me? Is there something I did to make life miserable? Or maybe something's wrong with Debbie. Maybe she's this impossible bitch who'll always drive men away. If either of those things are true, then Bradley's leaving could be the canary in the coal mine warning me of a perpetually shitty life. And things might actually be easier because I can go ahead and reset my expectations."

Julian thinks about this a moment, biting idly at his lip. Without making eye contact, he asks, "And what if neither is true? What if your stepdad left because sucky things happen sometimes for no reason?"

"I'd be relieved. It'd mean all the things that've happened so far could be chalked up to bad luck. And maybe by having such bad luck early on in life, I'm more likely to have good luck later. Maybe I'll win the lottery."

The Last Good Halloween

Julian laughs stoutly. A chill wind sweeps down the street corridor. I hunch my shoulders and turtle my neck into my coat collar.

"So?" I say, because I've laid out my argument, plus a good deal more than I'd expected or wanted. It's up to Julian now. He looks into the face of the oncoming wind and squints his eyes against the grit. There's a resoluteness to him that I've never seen before.

"So," he says. "That's it, I guess." And it's as close as I'm going to get to yes.

Thursday night I'm a model child with Debbie and Uncle Harley. I eat my dinner, share about my day, and listen and nod vigorously at appropriate intervals. After dinner and a polite amount of TV watching, I tell them I'm tired and that I have an early call at school the next morning to work on a biology group project. The whole evening goes so smoothly, I can tell they're almost sad to see me leave them there on the couch. And even I'm feeling a twinge of regret that life can't always be like this.

In my room, I go over the plan. I draw a neat line across *Item No. 1: Convince Julian to let me use his dad's car.* Then I go over the rest of it, wracking my brain to see if there are any weak items that don't hold up. They seem sound, so I pack my backpack with a few essentials that could come in handy on the road: 4 sticks of beef jerky; the letter Bradley sent to my mother; an envelope with $172 of lawn mowing cash; a plastic Mr. Pibb bottle filled with an unmeasured mixture of liquor; and a photograph of Debbie, me and Bradley taken after my junior high graduation, which I may need to use as an emotional carrot in case I meet any resistance.

Later on, as I lay in bed, the enormity of tomorrow's undertaking yawns wide before me. And as that dark unknown opens up and I peer into its depths, it's clear there are two possible paths my life can take in the morning. On the one hand, I could choose to wake up at my usual time, go to school like it's a normal day, toss out the plan I've spent the last week constructing. If I do that, I can also forget about Bradley coming home, get used to Uncle Harley and the instability that'll likely follow in his wake. In short, I could let my life unfold around me. That would be the safest option. But that would also be a compromise – the kind of easy deal you make that sets a tone, becomes a pattern, turns into a personality, and eventually makes you into the person you're going to be.

On the other hand, I could see my plan through.

In the end, there's really no choice.

Chapter 9

That night, I dream I'm fishing on the edge of a stagnant lake. The shore is overgrown with roots, and the trees hang out perilously over the brackish water. I'm reeling in my line when something takes it and dives for the bottom. No matter how hard I pull, I can't get it to budge. My only option is to keep reeling. As the line gets tighter, it makes little guitar string squeaks and paints cylindrical ripples on the surface. Just when it seems like it can't get any tighter and the line is about to give, I snap wide awake, out of breath and more tired than if I hadn't slept at all.

It's 5:15, and since my alarm was set for 5:30 anyway, I decide to just go ahead and take a shower to wake up. I turn the water on extra scalding hot to try and wash off the stink from my dream.

Back in my bedroom, Mr. T is sniffing warily at my ankles. He's finely attuned to my schedule, so he knows something is amiss. His ears are down and his stumpy tail is shaking. He wants to know if my plans include him.

"I'll be back soon, buddy," I whisper, giving him a quick head-scratch. "You're in charge 'til I get back."

He yawns, licks his beard and jumps onto my bed for a few more hours of shuteye. Once I'm dressed and ready to leave, I'm struck with a sense of incompleteness, of business left unfinished –

the way someone who has the noose around his neck and is about to tip the stool might suddenly realize he's forgotten to feed his goldfish. So I remind myself that I'm only going to be gone for a day. If everything works out, no one'll even notice my absence.

Outside, the porch is shrouded in inky blackness. I nearly jump out of my shoes when I notice that one of the nighttime shadows is a person standing to the left of the screen door.

"You're leaving a little early," Uncle Harley says. At first it looks like his breath is visible in the brisk morning air. Then I see a glowing ember between his fingers and realize he's smoking.

"I told you last night. I've got a biology group project to work on."

"It's still dark out," he says, flicking his ash over the porch railing.

"Does Debbie know you smoke? She can't be too fond of that habit."

"I hide nothing from your mother," he says with what seems like an implied threat.

"I'm stopping by my friend Julian's house on the way to school. He's working on the project with me."

"Why are you so jumpy?" he asks.

"I really should get going," I say, ignoring his question and cautiously placing my foot on the first porch step.

He takes a long drag on his cigarette and blows it out the side of his mouth. "I have to say I'm a little hurt, Kirby."

Somewhere inside me my gut twists around itself.

"I have a master's degree in biology. That's most of what I do at the beet refinery. You haven't even mentioned biology before last night. You never thought to ask for my help?"

"Yeah, but you probably deal with small stuff, like bacteria and viruses and stuff, right?"

"Mostly."

Cromley

"This project's on bigger animals. The kind you can see without a microscope."

"Megafauna. That's what we biologists call them, Kirby."

"Listen, Harley, if I don't pick up my friend and get to school, the group's going to be pissed."

"Sure thing," he says, stubbing his cigarette against the railing. He looks like he might flick the butt into the yard but then thinks better of it. "I'm serious about helping you with the biology. Maybe this weekend we'll sit down and put our heads together."

I launch myself down the rest of the steps. When I reach the sidewalk, I risk a look back. Uncle Harley's already inside. Feeling paranoid that he's wise to my ruse and has gone in to notify Debbie, or even the police, I take off sprinting towards Julian's house. Then I realize that a kid sprinting in the dark is likely to attract even more attention, so I force myself to walk. As I do so, I pull out my plan and cross off *Item No. 2: Sneak out early.*

Julian's house is bigger than mine. It's got a second floor and their basement is a finished rec room – though the Millers' term for it is "rumpus room," which is a phrase I can barely force myself to utter. All the windows are dark, with shades pulled down to the sills. From my sidewalk vantage point, the place looks abandoned, as if the owners had put it up for sale and moved out of town in a hurry.

Still, it's best to approach with caution. I scurry along the hedge that leads into the backyard. The bedrooms are upstairs, and Julian's, if my recollection of the floor plan is correct, is on the southwest side. I poke around 'til I find a dirt clod and do a soft underhand toss that barely nicks the window pane. The next throw is an overhand one that misses the window and hits the vinyl siding with a hollow thud. I jump into a boxwood shrub and wait with my breath held. Not even the faintest ripple of life comes from inside.

As I'm cocking my arm back for the third toss, I hear a whispered, "Hey," coming from somewhere near my feet. The voice is so quiet and low it sounds like a snake hissing. "Why are you throwing rocks at my parents' bedroom?"

"Julian?" His pale face is staring at me from the basement window well.

"I slept in the rumpus room last night," he says. "Give me a hand."

I lie on my belly and reach down into the darkness. The window tilts open and a moment later, Julian's cold hand seizes mine. Slowly, he emerges from the bowels of the basement and spills out into the backyard.

"You got the keys?" I ask, dusting myself off.

Julian pats his pocket and gestures for me to follow. He leads me into the alley. Some birds who haven't gotten the memo to fly south yet are starting to hungrily chirp themselves awake in a tree nearby. We walk a few lots down and come upon a detached garage behind an apartment building. It's a run-down structure with peeling paint and an overall rightward lean. Julian takes out a key ring and begins working on the padlock. I have to say, I'm impressed with his derring-do. I'd been expecting resistance, another battle to convince him to go through with it. Instead, it's almost as if he's taking over, and I'm the one tagging along. He eventually finds the right key and the lock springs open.

Inside, it's dark and warm and the air is suffused with the sweet smell of WD40. I can see the tarp-covered outline of a car.

"Give me a hand," Julian says as he grabs a corner of the tarp.

Two things are immediately apparent once we've gotten it uncovered. One, the car isn't exactly in mint condition. It's got cobwebs in the wheel wells, and the chrome accoutrements are developing a greenish patina. Frankly, it looks like we'll be lucky if this beast even runs. The second thing that jumps out at me is a problematic yellow racing stripe that runs up the center of the hood, over the roof, and down the tail. Julian never mentioned this cosmetic detail before, and I'm not pleased to be finding out about it now. This car is going to stand out even more than I'd feared. Of course there's no point mentioning this fact to Julian, who already has a skittish look in his eyes.

"Come on, let's go," he says, holding the keys out to me.

"Who's driving?" I ask. This is a point that's not covered in my plan, and I feel momentarily lost. "I only have my learner's permit, Julian."

I can't tell him that I haven't been behind a wheel since The Event, and that it might be nice if my very next driving experience wasn't also a criminal act.

Julian shakes his head. "I've only driven my parents' van before. This whole thing was your idea."

A neighbor across the alley lets their dog out and it starts barking in the near distance. The light outside the garage is turning gray. Billings is waking up and time is running out.

"Fuck it," I say, snagging the keys from his hand.

Because it's a tight fit in the garage, the doors only open a few inches, and we have to squeeze ourselves inside. The dashboard is covered in a thick layer of dust and I can detect the faint odor of mothballs. The vinyl seats are cold and hard as boards. The whole thing feels like it was designed for humans with vastly different proportions than mine.

I put the key in the ignition, hold my breath, and twist. The engine stammers for a few seconds, then reluctantly turns over. The exhaust burps a few oily clouds, and smooths out to an even thrum.

With a shaky hand, I slide the gearshift into D. I tap the gas pedal and the car leaps forward. It's out in the alley before I even have a chance to worry about hitting something. The engine is purring like a large, dangerous feline. Julian gets out, closes the garage door behind us and locks it.

This time, I barely even think about giving it gas and the car begins to roll forward. As the tires crunch down the gravel alleyway, I'm struck by the feeling that this machine, with its giant engine throbbing deep inside its chest, is fundamentally unstable – something I'm barely in control of.

"I brought a highway map in case you don't know how to get to Great Falls," Julian says once we've gotten a couple blocks away from his house.

"A few quick stops first."

"We didn't take this car so you could run errands, Kirby." He braces his hands against the dashboard as if he's expecting an impact. "Why are we heading toward school?"

"We're not going to school." I turn south down 3rd Street.

We drive for ten minutes in silence. With each block we pass, the houses get shabbier, the yards get more weed-choked, and the cars parked out front get older. I also notice a rise in the number of Dukakis yard signs, which puts me on edge, makes me feel like I'm entering hostile territory.

"Seriously, Kirby, where are you taking us?"

I pull out a piece of paper from my jacket pocket and hand it to Julian. He unfolds it and scans. At the top is the first part of a typing lesson, then, halfway down, the lesson stops mid-word and goes to:

```
Why do you need my address?
Does this "plan" involve me?
Shouldn't you have asked me first?
3612 S. Billings Blvd. #2F
Weirdo!
```

"Why didn't you tell me someone else was coming with?" Julian asks.

"Because you might not have gone through with it."

He bites his lip and stares straight ahead. I slow down and peer at the houses through the morning half-light. Number 3612 is a two-story apartment building with the fake stone siding that reminds me of *The Flintstones*. I pull the car over and put it into park.

"I'll be right back."

Cromley

Julian looks at me, then quickly at the keys dangling from the ignition. I debate taking them with me to make sure he doesn't bail, but it's probably a good idea to establish some trust, so I leave the car running and hop out.

The second I step onto the front walkway, a massive Rottweiler comes barreling out of the neighbor's house and bounds across its front yard, jaws blazing. Its bark is deep and demonic as it thrashes against the flimsy chain-link.

The building's entrance is nearly blocked by a drift of uncollected newspapers and phonebooks. Before I can hit the button for 2F, a buzzer sounds and I push the door open. The inside is cold and clammy, with gray carpet that's nearly worn threadless. The place is so depressing it almost makes me not want to go upstairs. It's difficult for me to imagine that Izzy lives in a place like this.

The door to her apartment is white, with a halo of black scuffmarks around the doorknob, as if someone had tried to kick it open on more than one occasion. I can hear voices behind it. I knock twice, quietly, afraid of what might be on the other side.

The door swings open and there, like a miracle, is Izzy. She's wearing an army surplus jacket, a short black skirt, and black tights with enough runners in them to make it seem intentional.

"I got off work three hours ago," she says, "so no comments about how I look, okay?"

"Why would I do that?"

"Come in." She throws the door open wide. "Don't worry. No one's here."

The apartment is as dingy as the hallway, with dark shag carpeting and dirty windows. The coffee table in the middle of the living room has last night's Chinese food cartons on it. Beyond that is the TV, which is the source of the voices I heard out in the hallway. Some kind of morning show is on and they're interviewing Vice President Bush. But the camera angle is unflattering, too tight and low. All you can see is a close-up view of his teeth, which are not in good shape.

There's nothing in the apartment I can really latch on to, no artwork on the walls, no quirky knick-knacks. Everything seems so temporary, so provisional. I wish there were something here, some clue to tell me who Izzy really is.

"I'm almost ready," she says as she slips on a pair of tall black boots and begins the process of lacing them up. "So what's this hush-hush mission all about?"

"Top secret plan," I say, drifting deeper into the apartment.

"Since I'm part of this plan, don't you think I should know a little something about it?"

"That's on a need-to-know basis," I tell her.

She's finished with one boot and now sets to work on the other. "I should warn you," she says, "I usually hate plans."

"This is a good one. And it's more of a checklist anyway."

"How does it turn out in the end?" She looks up from her lacing as she asks this, and it feels like she might be talking about something else.

"Essentially, the misunderstood loser proves his worth in the end," I say. "It's your basic Rudolph the Red-Nosed Reindeer story."

She nods for a moment, then finishes her lacing.

"Come here." I take her by the arm and lead her to the far window. "You see that car? We're taking it to Great Falls."

"To track down Bradley," she says with what I think is admiration.

I nod. "It belongs to my friend Julian's dad."

"You stole it?"

"Julian's with me, so it's not quite grand theft auto."

"Hmmm." She's standing so close I can feel the hum vibrate along my neck.

"You didn't think I'd actually follow through."

Cromley

Izzy retrieves an olive-green beret from the front closet and pulls it on at a jaunty angle that makes her seem like some kind of 60s radical.

Outside, when the neighbor's Rottweiler comes bounding up, she reaches into her pocket and pulls something out. "Easy, Boswell." She holds out a stick of string cheese. He sniffs it once, then eagerly inhales it.

"His name's Boswell?" I ask. "Like the guy on *Charlie's Angels*?"

"That would be Bos*ley*. And since you don't like me making literary references, I won't tell you who he's named after."

Boswell licks her hand and then rolls onto his back in a bid for her to work his belly.

"It's not his real name," she says, "but that's what I call him since his owners named him Rommel."

"Oh," I say, "at least I get that reference."

Boswell's enjoying his time with Izzy immensely and I'm not eager to rob him of it, but when I look up at the Roadrunner, I see Julian looking jumpy, like he might hop behind the wheel and abort this mission before it actually gets started.

"Izzy," I say.

"I know," she says. "I know. The plan."

Julian and Izzy have never met before. I can sense their unease with each other when I flip the seat forward and Izzy climbs in.

We stop at a Super America and I use the payphone to call in sick at school for Julian and me, altering my voice each time. When I offer to do the same for Izzy, she tells me she wasn't planning on going in today anyway.

Before I climb back into the car, I go over my checklist and draw lines through: *Item No. 3: Meet up with Julian; Item No. 4: Borrow Roadrunner; Item No. 5: Pick up Izzy;* and *Item No. 6: Call in sick to school.* It already feels like we're making progress.

The Last Good Halloween

"Hey," Julian says, "I just realized this is like that Ferris Bueller movie."

"Have you ever seen that movie?" I ask, knowing that PG-13 flicks are no-go in the Miller household.

"Not really," he admits.

"I can confidently tell you what we're doing is nothing like that movie. Not even close. This isn't some larky joyride. We're on a serious mission here."

Julian looks at the ground morosely as we climb into the car.

Pulling out of the gas station, the three of us are treated to a view of the sun creeping up from the plains to the east – a thin band of red and salmon that spans the horizon from the Rimrocks on the left, to as far south as the eye can see.

"Look at that," I say. "That's a good omen."

"Pretty," Izzy says from the backseat. "What's that saying about when the sky is red it's good or something?"

I pilot the Roadrunner onto 27th Street, heading toward Airport Hill, where we'll catch Highway 3 north toward Great Falls.

"Red sky at night, sailor's delight," Julian says. "Red sky at morning, sailors take warning."

"Oh," Izzy says and stretches out across the backseat. "Maybe not the best expression to apply here."

We've hit Airport Hill. The car is moving fast, and the engine hasn't even begun to work. Maybe it's what Julian said about sailors that's got me thinking of those old maps they made before they knew the world was round. The ones where the oceans are dotted with sea monsters and mermaids and whirlpools, and at the edges, it all just drops off into nothing. As the Roadrunner crests the hill and bucks forward, it feels as if we're in one of those old schooners, hurtling quickly toward the edge of the known universe.

Chapter 10

My only non-city driving session was the time Debbie let me do part of the drive to computer camp. Needless to say, the Roadrunner has a lot more muscle than Debbie's little four-cylinder Subaru. Toddling along on a two-lane highway at 55 MPH, this behemoth feels resentful that I'm not giving it a chance to flex its muscles.

The sound system in this rig is a stock radio with those old plastic punch-buttons. Since we're out of range of the Billings FM stations, Julian is slowly trolling through the AM band, ear cocked as he twists from one staticky cloud to the next. This being Montana, the stations that come in most clearly are Christian ones, which you can recognize right away by the singers' clean voices and solemn diction before you even make out the actual words. Whenever the dial alights on one of these perches, Julian looks over at me to ask if this one is all right. I give a quick head shake and he begins the search anew. I don't have anything personal against Christian music. I just find something so depressing about these salvation-peddling stations – mostly, I think, because of who they're intended to reach. Long-haul truckers, traveling salesmen, and the rest of life's lottery losers, relegated to nomadic existences on the country's back roads and byways. How lonely do you have to be to listen to someone singing about an entity that no one's even sure if it *exists*? Pretty goddamn lonely, I would imagine.

The terrain sliding by outside our windows is wide open and empty, almost characterless. Up ahead I can see isolated dark clouds with rain showers streaking toward the ground. They're silently moving east like ghosts roaming the flat earth.

Julian finds a station that's piping in classic country, and while I think that might be the second-most lonely radio format to listen to, it's shaping up to be our best option. I give him an approving nod and he leans back in his seat. The guy on the radio is singing about how he did wrong in life and how it wasn't his mama's fault because she tried to raise him better.

"Is everything okay in back?" I ask.

There's no answer, so I snatch a quick over-the-shoulder glance. Izzy's on her side, curled into a fetal semi-circle with her back toward us.

"I think she's asleep," Julian whispers.

"She worked late last night."

"Do you know where she works?" Something about the way he asks this makes me think he knows the answer.

"I think she's a waitress."

Julian slides his hands under his thighs and looks out the side window. "How well do you know her, Kirby?"

"She's in my typing class," I say. "Where does she work?"

"How should I know?"

"You sound like you do."

He leans toward the window and exhales so that a circle of fog appears on the glass for a few seconds then vanishes.

"I just heard once she works at Cattle Call." He says this quietly, almost reverently. With good reason.

Cattle Call is the only strip bar in Yellowstone County. Located fifteen miles outside Billings' city limits, it's tucked away off the interstate near a particularly run-down section of the notoriously run-down suburb of East Laurel. I've never been there before, but I've heard of it. Everyone has. It's supposedly this Petri dish of sudden violence, illicit drugs, and commodified sex.

"That sounds like another one of your mother's church rumors," I say. Christian groups are always trying to mobilize various petitions against its existence, although so far they've never managed to shut it down.

"Actually, I heard it from a kid in my Spanish class whose older brother saw her there."

"I doubt it," I say. Though I have to admit this would explain Izzy's secrecy about her place of employment. It could, in fact, explain a lot of things.

I steal another glance behind me and notice that the hem of her army jacket is riding up slightly, revealing a meringue-colored slice of skin. There's a tiny black mole right where her left kidney resides. And it's entirely possible, as I gaze into the shadowy gap where the waistband of her jeans pulls away, that that's a miniscule sliver of underwear I'm seeing right now. With only that as a stimulus, I've already sprouted a full-mast boner.

"Hey careful, Kirby," Julian says.

By the time I rip my eyes back to the road, the car has drifted over the centerline. My hands tighten around the steering wheel and I ease us back into our lane. I squeeze my eyes shut hard for a second, trying to purge the image from my brain, but it only seems to set it further. My tongue is itchy. My hands are slick. I wish to God I would have jerked off last night when I had the chance – one of those little precautions you forget to take that can come back to haunt you.

Unable to stop myself, I turn again to take in that tiny miracle of skin and fabric. This time, Julian follows my stare and he, too, basks in the glow. It's like some rare gift – way better than any of the pictures in my book, because this is the real, breathing thing.

The Last Good Halloween

It isn't until I hear the sound of gravel kicking up against the undercarriage that I'm able to pull myself away. The right wheels have strayed onto the shoulder. When I try to bring them back onto the road, I overcorrect and the tail kicks out to the right. Dimly recalling something from driver's ed, I steer into the skid. The car rocks back and forth and the wheels give off a series of short, rubber-burning squeals before I manage to get us going straight again.

The commotion is enough to jostle Izzy awake. I hear her murmur and roll over. A moment later she yawns and appears in the rearview mirror.

"What's with the turbulence, Captain?" Her voice is husky with sleep. Her beret is cocked at an angle that makes her seem more like a French tourist than a revolutionary dissident. "How long was I out?"

"Maybe an hour." Julian turns in his seat so he's facing her. "Feel better?"

There's a rustling sound as Izzy digs through her jacket pockets. "Anyone mind if I smoke?" she asks, holding up a crushed pack of Camels.

"Not a good idea," I say, trying to seize her gaze in the rearview mirror. "We're not out for a joyride. We've got to stay focused on the mission at hand."

"How does a cigarette detract from our mission?"

"Plus, it'll smell up Julian's dad's car."

Izzy frowns at me. "Since it's his dad's car, why don't you let Julian answer for himself?"

"I don't want him to feel like he has to let you, that's all."

Julian bites his lips. I can tell he doesn't want to come off as uncool in front of this new person who obviously outcools him by a long stretch.

"The smell'll be long gone by the time we get back to Billings," Izzy presses. "It's not that big of a deal."

Cromley

Julian's eyes search the car nervously. He rubs his hands on his kneecaps.

"Here's the thing," I say, trying to save him. "I'm not opposed to smoking because of the smell or because I'm a prude. I'm against it because it's such a cliché, such an obvious teenage affectation. Everyone's doing it simply because it's understood that this is how we're supposed to rebel against our elders."

No one says anything.

"It's like we've been issued some Teenage Field Manual. And everyone thinks they have to follow it. I hate that idea. That's why I'll enjoy a cocktail every once in a while in the privacy of my own home, but you'd never catch me at a kegger."

"Have you ever been invited to a kegger?" Julian asks.

"That's not the point."

"So you're against being social when it comes to vices," Izzy says.

"Kind of," I say. "But it's more the conformity aspect of it that irks me. You see what I mean?"

Again, the car goes quiet.

Julian turns in his seat to look at Izzy. "If you want to smoke, you can."

"That's okay, pal," she says, re-stowing her cigarettes. "Kirby really knows how to take the fun out of something. He'll invite you to a pool party, then go ahead and drain the pool."

Julian giggles. That last line felt like a cheap shot.

"So, Izzy," I say, "you were working late last night?"

"Yeah."

"Where is it you work again?"

Julian, hearing my question, stops giggling.

"Nowhere," she says. And then, perhaps aware of how ridiculous that sounded, she adds, "You've never heard of the place."

"If it's open late at night, it must be some kind of tavern or bar or something."

The Last Good Halloween

Julian squirms uncomfortably. There's a long pause from the backseat. When I check the mirror, Izzy is looking at me with a hard stare.

"Not necessarily," she says at last. "My job could be restocking grocery store shelves. It could be the late shift at a bakery. I could be an orderly at a hospital. I could be a janitress cleaning out business offices. Or maybe—"

"I get it," I say.

"Of course, I know there *are* rumors out there," she says. "I'm aware of what's been said about me."

"You are?" Julian would make an awful poker player.

"You didn't hear the one about me in orchestra class last year?"

Julian and I both say no at the same time.

"I'm surprised. It was kind of a big deal." She does a couple idle flicks of her lighter. "Start by saying I used to be pretty good at the viola. Not a prodigy or anything, but I might've been good enough to get a scholarship if I'd stuck with it."

Her voice has gone flat and I'm having a hard time reading her tone.

"One day I go in early before school to pick up some new strings. Right? No big deal because kids usually hang out in the orchestra room before school. Only that day no one was there, except Mr. Tanner, who was back in his office."

She pauses, either to make sure her thoughts are in order, or possibly for dramatic effect. I've got a heavy feeling in my gut as I wait for her to continue.

"Anyway, to keep it short, he pulled out his wang and showed it to me."

"No way," Julian says.

Izzy nods, tight-lipped. "He was fully erect. And he basically made it clear that he wanted me to, you know, *service* him."

"What happened?"

"Here's the really awful part. I reported it to the principal and they started to investigate, but somehow Tanner got it flipped around so they started asking *me* questions, like it was *my* fault. What was I wearing that morning? Why was I in there before school?"

"That sucks," Julian says as if the thought had never occurred to Izzy before.

"Then the rumors started up. I was having an affair with him. He gave me AIDS. We were engaged. I'd gotten into a knife fight with his wife. I was having his baby."

"I don't remember hearing any of those," I say.

"Trust me, they were out there."

Julian asks, "So what happened?"

"If my mom were even a remotely decent mother she would have pulled me out of that school in a heartbeat." Izzy flicks her lighter a couple more times. "But I think deep down she didn't believe me either. So I stopped playing the game. Quit orchestra. Found some new people to hang out with who didn't give a shit one way or the other."

She leans back in her seat and extends her feet between Julian and me. "Made life a million times easier."

I've got a hunch there may be some embellishments to her story, though I know she quit orchestra last year, so enough of it's true that I can't call bullshit outright. That may sound cold, but you could hardly blame me for being cynical when you realize, as I just did, that once again she's managed to dodge the question of where she works. And she did it in a way where if I do press the issue, I'd come off as a hopeless asshole. Clever Izzy.

"That explains a lot," I conclude, trying to sound at least a little skeptical.

She nods and flicks her lighter a couple more times.

I turn the radio up as some cowboy yodels about herding cattle, and I happily lose myself for a while trying to decide if he's singing about herding the cattle metaphorically, and if so what the metaphor might represent. By the time the song's over, I've concluded there's no metaphor. Herding is just herding, and cattle are just cattle.

"We need gas," I say.

They're the first words anyone has uttered in a good thirty minutes. No one seems eager to chime in.

"That looks like a place up ahead." I point with my chin at a gas station set back on the gravel frontage road.

It's one of those non-franchise stations with a tiny square shack and two pump islands out front. The sign says *Stu's Stopover*, and you get the impression there's probably a real Stu who's obese and wears grease-stained overalls and who cheerfully logs most of the hours behind the till. I flip the blinker and ease off the gas. I've been on road trips with Debbie and Bradley and stopped at rural gas stations hundreds of times, but it's a different feeling when it's *you* that's pulling into one of these distant way stations. You're filled with an overwhelming sense of gratitude that someone has thought to locate their place of business right here, as if they'd been anticipating your needs and had done it solely for your benefit.

By the time I execute the turn, I'm positively buoyant, and not even the temporary marquee that – either belatedly or very prematurely – reads "Hap y 4 July" can bring my spirits down. No, what grabs me and smacks me back to reality is that I don't know where the gas tank is located. I pull the car to a stop before committing to one side or the other. When I ask Julian where it is, he shrugs his shoulders and says, "How should I know?"

I get out and take a lap around the car. By the time I get to the passenger window I've been unable to locate anything that looks like a gas tank. I tap on the glass. "I can't find it."

Julian says, "Beats me."

Cromley

"I can't believe you never paid attention when your dad filled it. Did you think it was solar-powered?"

Izzy says, "I know on some cars it's behind the license plate."

Though the notion seems farfetched, it turns out, upon inspection, she's right. Once I've got the hose set and filling, I take snack orders from Julian and Izzy and head inside.

The door has a bell attached to it that gives off a lazy jingle when I muscle it open. The guy behind the counter does not look how I pictured Stu – if he's even Stu at all. This guy has close-cropped orange hair and a twitchy face. He's got jug ears, one of which he's unwisely chosen to accentuate with a hugely fake diamond stud.

"Morning," I twang. "How goes it?"

He doesn't respond, just follows me with a pair of shifty gray eyes as I walk the aisles. There's not much to choose from so I end up getting Izzy a Sunkist, and Julian a 7-Up and a bag of off-brand potato chips. For me, a Styrofoam cup of coffee that's boiled down so long in its carafe that it has a measurable viscosity. I'm not a coffee drinker, per se, but I'm needing a caffeine infusion and this feels like the right time to take up the habit.

The counter guy – who I'd place in his mid-twenties – glances over the merchandise when I set it down and says something I can't make out.

"Excuse me?"

"*That be all*?" he says, this time hostilely over-enunciating in the way Americans usually reserve for communicating with foreigners.

"Yes, thank you. And the gas."

He punches some numbers on the cash register.

"Kinda car's that?" The question seems friendly enough, though you can never be too sure. The truth is a risk. A lie seems even riskier.

"Roadrunner," I say.

He looses a low-decibel whistle. "What year's it?"

The Last Good Halloween

"Sixty-nine."

He frowns and punches in the last price and hits total. "Been driving it long?"

He's officially crossed the line between idle curiosity and outright snoopiness. And, stupid me, I waited too long to catch it. Now I'm boxed in. If I say a long time, he'll ask why I couldn't find the gas tank. If I say not long, that opens the door on a whole series of further questions whose answers only dig a deeper hole for myself.

I fish a twenty from my wallet and hold it out across the counter. He makes no move for the money. His eyes settle on me as if to let me know he wants an answer before he'll finish the transaction.

I give him a devilish smile and a quick double-pump of my eyebrows. "Funny you should ask, I just stole it this morning, hoss."

For a few seconds, nothing. And then, so quickly it could almost be confused for a twitch, the corners of his mouth pull wide and he unleashes a high-pitched whinny.

He takes my twenty and the cash register drawer shoots open with a resounding ping. The mood is suddenly light. We've formed a bond, this red-headed attendant and me. If we were at a bar, we might indulge in a game of darts, or a round of manly arm-wrestling. It just goes to show there's no chasm that can't be crossed.

I'm feeling so good about how it's turned out that I decide there's one more piece of business I'd like to take care of before we hit the road – something that will ensure my mind is in the right place going forward.

"Think I'll use the facilities," I say, scooping up the change.

"It's around back," he says, "through that side door." He hands me a key, which is chained to a foot-long piece of two-by-four.

The bathroom is unisex, and it smells so strongly of mildew and bleach that I can feel it scalding my sinuses. The toilet seat is down, sprinkled with flecks of yellow pee. I'm not a fan of road games, but this is important, for the long term good of the mission. I wad up a nest of toilet paper and unbutton my jeans. I start off thinking of Izzy sleeping in the back of the Roadrunner, but the image lacks the potency it had a few minutes ago. So I switch channels to Izzy in the wooden playground fort, calling me to join her in the tower. This one starts to work. I can feel myself getting a semi-chub. So I go with the fantasy, me climbing the tower, me finding her naked up there, her taking my finger and putting it in her mouth – but then I accidentally open my eyes and catch sight of myself in the bathroom mirror, which is something you never, ever want to see when you're doing this. It's a setback.

I close my eyes and regroup. Start with an image of Izzy and she's not wearing anything except for—

"Dude, come on! Can't you read?"

This is not Izzy's fantasy voice – it's an actual voice, coming from a speaker mounted above the door. Next to it is a sign: "These facilities are for number one and two ONLY! All other uses will be prosecuted to the fullest extent of the law."

I'm frozen. I can't move – not even to let go of my dick and put it back in my pants.

"How do you know what I'm doing?" I ask, my voice sounding oddly prayer-like in the empty bathroom.

"You know I have to clean that up when my shift's over," the speaker says. "Highly inconsiderate."

I still don't know if he knows what I was doing, so I try bluffing. "I'm just going to the bathroom, man."

"You're not the first person who's spanked his monkey in there. And you won't be the first person we've charged for a sex crime either."

He knows everything. They even have an established legal protocol. All at once, a post-embarrassment blood-rush kicks in. My body thaws and quickly overheats so that a prickly sweat breaks out.

The Last Good Halloween

I've lost most of my fine motor skills, but I just manage to button my pants back up. I ease the door open and slip outside.

Peeking into the station through the side door, I can see the attendant watching a black-and-white closed circuit TV. He looks up from it and flashes me a lascivious smile. I'm pretty sure their surveillance system is illegal, but it's not as if I'm in a position to file a police report right now, not after being caught red-handed, as it were.

"I bet your friends out there might like to know what you were up to," the attendant chirps. He makes a stylized jerking off gesture with his hand and guffaws.

I've heard enough.

I bolt around the side of the building to see Izzy giving Julian smoking lessons, seemingly unaware of my predicament or the fact that they're standing over a massive underground reservoir of gasoline.

"Get in the car!" I call out.

"What's the matter?"

I slash a finger across my throat and keep speed walking. Izzy must read something in my body language because she drops the cigarette and begins herding Julian. As I'm rounding the front bumper, I'm vaguely aware of the gas station door opening behind me.

I turn the key and the engine thunders reassuringly to life, like a horse that shows up at the exact right moment to rescue the hero from certain doom. Feeling a little safer now, I hazard a glance back.

The red-haired guy is waving both hands over his head as if he forgot to tell me something, and wants me to wait. I throw the gearshift into D. I crunch my foot down on the gas. The Roadrunner lurches, hesitates for a second, then launches forward.

"Kirby, what's going on?" Izzy asks. "You forgot our drinks."

"That guy was mad you were smoking so close to the pumps," I say.

Cromley

"We weren't *that* close," she says. "What an asshole."

"Exactly," I say.

"Kirby," Julian says.

"Trust me, he was really pissed off."

"Kirby," he says again. "What's that noise?"

That's when I notice it too – an arrhythmic thunk-thunk coming from somewhere behind us.

"Holy shit!" Izzy's turned around, looking out the back window. "Kirby, stop the car."

"I can't. That guy was super pissed."

"Seriously, Kirby, you just—"

It is in this exact nanosecond I realize what I've done, rendering the rest of what Izzy will say unnecessary. Of course, she has no way of knowing that I already know, so she continues:

"—yanked the hose off the pump!"

Anticipating the second half of her sentence, I've already shifted my foot to the brake pedal. The car bucks to a halt on the gravel and Izzy, unprepared for the sudden momentum shift, tumbles forward. Julian hasn't moved, only dug his fingers claw-like into his thighs. He appears to be frozen in a forward-facing stare. The shallow nose-breaths he's taking are the only real sign he's alive.

I get out and walk around back. Trailing from the gas tank is the black rubber pump hose, looking like a freshly snipped umbilical cord. The license plate hinge is bent, so I have to wrench the nozzle pretty good to get it out. When I do, a little amniotic gas leaks out onto the dusty gravel.

The orange-haired guy is standing at the edge of the station property, about twenty yards away. I hold the lifeless hose up in both hands.

"It was an accident!" I shout.

In his left hand, he's got a cordless phone. He looks at it a moment.

The Last Good Halloween

"Did you hear me? It was an accident! And I'm sorry about the bathroom thing."

He begins dialing a number on the phone.

I throw the hose down. A moment later, we're peeling out, tires spitting gravel and smoke in the general direction of Stu's Stopover.

Chapter 11

After a few minutes of white-knuckling it, I ease off the gas and bring us back down to the anonymity of the speed limit. No one's said anything since the gas station. I'm happy to let them think I'm upset that they were smoking near the pumps, though the reality is I'm quiet because I expect to see blue lights appear any second in the rearview mirror, or a road trap pop up around the next curve.

Fifteen minutes after our hasty departure from Stu's Stopover, Julian asks, "How bad is my dad's car messed up?"

His face is pale, his brow low and furrowed. He seems so tiny on the seat next to me. It's not just that I think he'll have a hard time hearing the truth. I think he'll have a hard time hearing the best possible spin I could put on the truth.

"Not bad," I tell him, fingers invisibly crossed.

"What does 'not bad' mean?"

"I don't know, Julian. It was a subjective question so I gave you a subjective answer."

I take a quick look at Izzy in back to see if she can offer any assistance. She's staring out the side window, indifferent to our conversation. If I had to guess, I'd say she's regretting her decision to come on this trip, maybe regretting ever talking to me in the first place.

The Last Good Halloween

"I want to see it," Julian says.

"That's impossible right now, buddy."

He clears his throat. "I mean it, Kirby. Pull over."

"We need to put some distance between us and that gas station." I tighten my grip on the wheel and make a show of focusing on the road.

"Pull over!" His voice comes out as a screech. "Now! Pull over now!" His face has gone violet; his eyes are two dark slits. He's worked up, and he's clearly not going to calm down on his own. Part of me's worried he might grab the steering wheel and yank if I don't give in.

"For Christ's sake," Izzy yells from the backseat, "let the kid see what happened to the car."

"Fine," I say. "I just saw a sign for a rest stop in two miles. Would anyone mind if I waited 'til then to pull over?"

Julian tucks his elbows in tight and turns to face forward. The radio is playing a Dolly Parton song where she sings in a voice that's supposed to sound like a little kid, but mostly it just comes across as creepy.

Thankfully, the rest stop is set a good fifty yards off the highway, leaving most of the parking lot shielded from view. The only other car here is a rusted-out Blazer that looks like it hasn't been moved in a while. The rest stop has a feel of off-season desolation, the kind of place where you could be murdered and remain undiscovered for a long time. As such, it's probably not the worst place in the world for us to regroup. I nose the Roadrunner into a spot near the cinderblock restroom facilities and turn it off.

Julian lets out a deep breath and opens the door. I get out and meet him at the back bumper.

"Oh my God." It's barely a whisper, almost inaudible.

The license plate frame is bent, and one of its hinges is ripped out from the chrome. In the cosmic scheme of things, the damage isn't *that* bad, but it's clearly disfigured.

Cromley

Julian falls to his knees and starts worrying his hands over the damage. His face has crumpled in on itself.

"Julian, buddy, it's going to be okay."

"Okay?!" he shouts. "Right now this is the opposite of okay." It's official. He's crying – big heaves from deep in his diaphragm making him struggle to keep his breath.

As I look over the rest of the vehicle, I notice the gas cap – by some miracle of physics – has wedged itself between the bumper and the lip of the trunk.

"Look! We still have the gas cap. What are the odds?"

His only answer is a series of wracking sobs, so I stoop over and twist the cap back on. "Trust me. We can fix this."

"How?" He's still on his knees, face streaked with tears, snot gurgling in his nostrils.

"Your dad takes this car out, what, three times a year? If that. Plus he parks it with the back end in. So when we get home this afternoon, we park it like normal and he won't notice a thing."

Julian starts to say something, but I hold up a finger to stop him.

"I've got a bunch of lawn mowing money saved up. Next week we'll take it in to get it fixed, then we put it back, good as new. No one knows a thing."

Julian keeps looking at me. His chest is still heaving, but his sniffling has subsided. It's clear he wasn't expecting me to have such a good strategy already figured out.

"That might work," he says.

I have to admit I'm a little surprised myself. It actually does sound feasible. Of course, he has no way of knowing my more immediate concern, which is the fact that our pal back at the gas station has likely contacted the authorities to report a renegade black Plymouth Roadrunner with a ridiculous yellow racing stripe being driven by a crazed sex-criminal. But I see no good in pointing this out just as Julian's starting to feel better.

The Last Good Halloween

He stands up and brushes the gravel off his knees. He notices Izzy leaning against the rear quarter panel and becomes self-conscious. He wipes his nose with the back of his hand. "I think I better..." He gestures with his thumb toward the bathroom. "I'll be out in a minute."

Once he's inside, I turn to look at Izzy. Her arms are crossed and she's tapping the toe of her boot rapidly.

"What?"

She doesn't say anything. Her mouth has shrunk into a short, straight line.

"Don't look at me like this is *my* fault," I tell her. "I'm not the one who was smoking at the gas station."

"That's not what I'm pissed about."

"I never would have ripped that hose off if you hadn't made me rush to get out of there."

She makes a clicking sound in the back of her throat, then looks away. Since she doesn't seem ready to tell me why she's mad, I set about trying to twist the license plate frame back into shape.

"I heard what you said about me in the car," she hisses.

"What?"

"About where I work."

"Wait a minute. I didn't say anything. It was Julian."

"I hate, hate, hate rumors, Kirby." She says this slowly, deliberately, still looking away.

"Right now I've got bigger concerns. Okay? Besides, you should be happy. The fact that they make up rumors about you means you're relevant. No one would even bother to make up a rumor about me."

She twists her mouth sideways. "Do you think I'm a stripper?" she asks. "Do you think I work at Cattle Call."

I shrug noncommittally.

"Answer the question, Kirby."

134

"I'm kind of preoccupied with not getting caught by the cops, Izzy."

"If you hear someone say something like that about your friend, you should defend them. Just like if I heard a rumor about you, I'd say it's not true."

It's hopeless trying to reshape the license plate frame so I stand back up. "When you don't tell me where you work, it does raise suspicions. You understand that, right?"

"If you were a real friend, it wouldn't matter."

"If you were a real friend, you'd tell me."

She drops her arms to her sides and squares her shoulders. She's looking at me now, eyes staring straight into mine in a way that's almost threatening. "You can be a real dick sometimes."

"I'm sorry," I say.

She takes a long, deep breath and re-crosses her arms. "Apology not accepted. You're just as bad as everyone else." She looks around quickly to survey her surroundings. "Now," she says, holding her hand out, "give me the keys."

"What for?"

"If you ever want to be my friend, give me the keys to the car."

She looks tired, like she's had enough of this adventure and wants to be done with it. The odds are pretty good if I give her the keys she'll take off. Which is probably what I deserve anyway.

I pull the keys from my pocket, dangle them for a second above her outstretched palm, then let go. Izzy flashes a fake smile and climbs into the car.

"Are you just going to leave us here?" I ask, as the motor thunders to life.

She doesn't hear me or pretends not to, then throws the car into gear. She begins cruising toward the exit to get back onto the highway. Just before she reaches it, though, she flips a U-turn and pulls up next to the rusted-out Blazer at the far end of the lot. She gets out of the car and circles around to the back, where she pops the trunk and begins rummaging around. I don't bother to ask what she's doing because I doubt she'd answer anyway.

A moment later, she stands up and begins efficiently unscrewing the Blazer's license plates. It only takes a minute for her to swap them out. When she's done, she takes the Roadrunner's plates and tosses them into the trunk and wipes her hands on her black skirt.

She surveys the rest stop, then climbs back into the car. This time, she drives past me, toward the picnic area. The Roadrunner hops the curb and rolls to a halt in the middle of a desolate patch of scrub grass where you're supposed to let your pets do their business.

"What are you doing?" I shout, even though the windows are rolled up and there's no chance she can hear me.

The RPMs jump twice as she flicks the gas; then the rear wheels start spinning at full throttle. The car surges and the tires start spinning. The engine lets out a redline scream. The tailpipe belches blue smoke. After a few seconds, the car is engulfed in a cloud of dust and grit.

Eventually, the engine goes calm and the Roadrunner emerges from the cloud. Izzy dips it off the curb, back into the lot. During the commotion Julian has come racing out of the bathroom, just in time to catch a lungful of dirt that leaves him doubled-over, hacking.

Izzy re-parks the Roadrunner and steps out. The car is now coated with a fine layer of dust. You can still tell it's black with a yellow stripe, but it doesn't stand out nearly as much.

"It was a little tricky getting the rear plate on, because of the damage," she says, "but it should hold."

"Not bad work," I say. "Not perfect, but not bad."

"I'd be happy with a simple thank you, Kirby."

"Thank you."

She tosses the keys to me and I snatch them out of the air.

Cromley

"The only direction is forward," she says. "Now let's get going."

"We'll wash it before we put it back," I say to Julian, who's stopped coughing and now is just staring with his jaw hanging open.

His purple lips curl into a shaky, reluctant smile. "Yeah," he says, "it looks like we'll need to."

Chapter 12

As the Great Falls city limits sign approaches and the first half of our journey officially comes to a close, I'm able to report that we have some good news, some bad news, and some neutral news.

The good news is that we've made it to Great Falls without being arrested. Granted, we haven't seen a single cop since the gas station debacle, so I can't say if our lack of incarceration is due to Izzy's improvised automotive camouflage or simply a matter of dumb luck.

The bad news is that it's a little after one o'clock. I never assigned a timeline to the items on my checklist. But a one o'clock completion of *Item No. 7 Drive to Great Falls* is well behind even my most pessimistic scenarios. If we turn around by two, we might not make it back to Billings until five, which could require us to invent some kind of secondary excuse to sell our parents. Neither of my companions has mentioned the fact that time is quickly slipping away from us, but they can read a clock as well as me.

The neutral news is that I'm starving. Right now my stomach is imploding in on itself with the force of a dying star. Judging by the lethargy of my fellow travelers, they, too, are nursing perilously low blood sugar levels. Unfortunately, because of the aforementioned bad news, there's not much we can do at the moment to take care of the neutral news. Then again, if you really want to look closely at this update, the fact that I've put not-getting-arrested into the *good* news column should tell you something about the unfriendly news cycle we happen to find ourselves in right now.

"Did you know," Izzy says, "that we are currently surrounded by nuclear missile silos?"

"Mmm-hmm," Julian says hazily.

"Did you also know that if Montana were to secede from the United States today, we'd be the third largest nuclear power behind the Soviet Union and America?"

Julian doesn't say anything to this and I have to admit I'm only half listening. As soon as we crossed the city limits I went into DEFCON 2, scanning every face, double-checking every car to make sure they don't belong to Bradley.

"Okay," Izzy says after a prolonged silence, "I get it. No one's interested in my nuclear trivia. But you *should* be. If World War III started today, we'd be at the epicenter of the first attack. Nothing to do here but kiss our asses good-bye."

As the Roadrunner noses deeper into the city, it becomes apparent that Great Falls is the kind of town that's most alive at its edges – a thin crust of mini-malls, car dealerships, and chain restaurants. Inside the city itself, there's an inordinate number of pawnshops, bail bondsmen, and adult bookstores. Once we reach the actual downtown, it's lifeless, the kind of place where you wouldn't be surprised to see tumbleweeds blowing across the road in front of you.

"So where's this stepfather of yours?" Izzy asks.

My grip on the steering wheel tightens involuntarily. The actual *where* of Bradley is the weakest element of the whole plan. I think I secretly knew this all along, but now that the next item is *No. 8: Find Bradley*, there's no denying it.

"I assume he's staying with his sister."

"You *assume*?" Izzy says, with just a touch of alarm.

Cromley

"Nothing in life is a hundred percent," I say. "Uncertainty is all around us." I sweep my hand across the blighted cityscape as if to illustrate this.

"Where does his sister live?" Julian asks.

"I don't have the exact address, but I remember the feel of where she lived."

Now that we're here, I can see how naïve I was to assume I'd just be able to *feel* my way to her house, which I've been to all of once. Still, admitting this now would be owning up to a level of cluelessness so breathlessly deep that my companions may begin to question the very nature of this undertaking. So I have no choice but to carry on like I know what I'm doing. Which, in some weird way, I'm realizing may be one of the galvanizing principles of adulthood.

"It's in the city proper," I say, "and it's this kind of plain neighborhood where all the houses look the same."

Izzy and Julian are silent, unable to find the right words to interrupt me.

"Her house is kind of white stucco and there's a blue one on the left and a yellowish one two doors to the right. Very distinct. You can't miss it."

I turn down a residential street that seems to fit the general profile of what I remember.

"What do you think it'll be like when you see your stepdad?" Julian asks, probably just to change the subject.

"Pretty weird, I guess. He'll probably be surprised to see me."

"What are you going to say?"

Though I didn't think it was possible, Julian's question causes my stomach to compact on itself even further. "I'm not exactly sure," I say, and this admission draws another lengthy silence from the car. I can't blame them. If they were to look at my plan they'd see *Item No. 9: Convince Bradley to come home.* That's it. No specifics, no details – it's a script that's all stage directions and no dialogue.

"It's pretty obvious I'll just tell him to come back home."

The Last Good Halloween

"Sure," Izzy says, "but have you thought about the tone you want to take? Like do you want to be confrontational? Or play sad, or what?"

We've reached the end of what seemed a promising street without seeing anything that looked remotely like Bradley's sister's house. I cut west for a block and begin prowling down another potential avenue.

"I brought a picture of the three of us from when I graduated junior high. I might break that out and use it on him."

"So kind of play the Little Orphan Kirby routine," she says.

"That's what feels the most natural," I say. "Is there anything wrong with that?"

"What do you think, Julian?" Izzy asks, poking him in the shoulder.

"I don't know," he says. "It seems kind of obvious, I guess."

"Right. Exactly. It's very obvious, Kirby."

"Then what would you guys do?" This parsing of my approach with Bradley is not helping my confidence.

"If you want him to come back, you have to give him some positive inducement. What's in it for him?"

"Yeah," Julian says, though I doubt he even knows what the word *inducement* means.

We've fruitlessly reached the end of what seemed like another promising block. When I cut over to the next street, though, it finally feels like we're on the right one.

"Think of what Bradley really enjoyed about living with you guys," Izzy says. "Something he maybe misses. That's the wedge you'll use to split him open."

"Yeah," Julian says again. His near-constant siding with Izzy is starting to get on my nerves, but it's too much to contemplate right now as I try to come up with something Bradley actually enjoyed about his life with us – a task that's proving to be harder than I would've guessed.

Cromley

Bradley always struck me as a pretty simple man – not simplistic, more what you'd call efficient. He was the kind of guy who didn't have a lot of outsized wants or passions, none of those things that can tie you down and possibly even hold you back in life. This fact is probably what impressed me most about Bradley, and also what apparently made it so easy for him to imagine his life in a completely different way, without Debbie and me.

"Did he have any hobbies?" There's a note of sympathy in Izzy's voice when she asks this.

"He liked magic."

"Okay, that's a start. Did he do magic with you or Debbie?"

"I used to. But not for a couple years." Suddenly, that day I told him I wasn't interested in magic anymore looms as a pivotal historical moment, fraught with ill consequences I never could've foreseen at the time.

"Is there anything else you guys had in common?"

"We're both big fans of Reagan," I say.

"That could be something," Izzy says, though I catch her frowning in the mirror when she doesn't know I'm looking.

We've reached the end of the street, and, again, I didn't see anything that looked like Bradley's sister's house. When we get to the next street over it's a commercial strip, dotted with fast food chains and muffler repair shops.

"Kirby, where does this sister live?" Julian asks.

"I thought it was right around here."

"Good Christ!" Izzy roars. "Pull into that gas station. What's his sister's name?"

"Edna. Edna Kellogg."

Izzy pushes Julian's seat forward and hops out of the car. She lifts up the plastic-covered phone book dangling beneath the booth and flips through the white pages for a minute. When she finds something, she tears the page from the book. Then she skips to the front and rips out the city map.

The Last Good Halloween

"Her name is Edina, by the way," Izzy says once she's climbed back into the car. "Not Edna."

I can hear the onionskin phone book pages crinkling as she studies them for a moment. Then:

"Go right down Central Avenue. She lives across the river. We weren't even close."

Edina's block, when we finally *do* get to it, looks exactly the way I'd pictured it, though admittedly it would've taken days to find it without Izzy's directions. I pull the Roadrunner to a halt on the opposite side of the street under the leafless fingers of a middle-aged elm.

"It looks kind of empty," Julian says.

Edina's house is a white stucco rectangle set back in a patchy yard that's rife with crabgrass. The front door is in the center of the house with one tiny window on either side. The whole place has an almost painful adherence to symmetry – it's quite possibly the most nondescript structure I've ever seen in my life. Not an ounce of soul or texture. No wonder I couldn't wait to get out of here the time we visited. And now that I'm seeing it again and confirming my earlier childhood suspicions about it, I wonder why on earth Bradley would come *here* in his quest to sort out his life. This is not the kind of place where you'd want to do a lot of heavy emotional calisthenics.

The Roadrunner's engine ticks and cools and I look out across the yard. All at once it hits me full-force in the solar plexus that the next conversation I engage in will have a disproportionate say in how the rest of my life plays out, the way some people might view an acceptance or rejection to their preferred university. And as this dawns on me, my stomach and all my other organs begin to expand uncontrollably.

"Are you ready, Kirby?" Julian asks.

The air is being forced out of my enlarging lungs and I can't seem to take any new air in, so I give my head a tight shake.

144

Cromley

"What are you thinking right now?" Izzy reaches her hands over the seat back and rests them on my shoulders. "You want us to leave you alone for a minute?"

There's no more air to force out, yet my lungs still feel like they're expanding.

"You never should have asked him what he was going to say," I hear Izzy hiss at Julian. "It completely messed him up."

"How was I supposed to know?" Julian says. "Besides, you talked about it too. It wasn't just me."

Their words seem as if they're being spoken from far off. It's oddly reassuring to hear yourself talked about as if you're not in the room. It makes you feel like you have some larger relevance that exceeds your immediate orbit – which I think might be a feeling that most people spend a good part of their lives and labors striving for.

My lungs are pressing hard against my ribcage. They've got no more room to expand. I just manage to steal a tiny gulp of air and with it, I blurt:

"Backpack."

"What did he say?" Izzy asks. "Bappa?"

"Say it again," Julian says. "What was that?"

"Backpack."

"I think he wants his backpack."

"Christ, he's turning blue. Hurry up!"

Julian scrambles out, pops the trunk and lays the backpack on my lap when he returns. I pull the zipper open and fish around inside until I find the Mr. Pibb bottle.

"I think he wants me to open it," Julian says.

"Are you sure, Kirby?" Izzy asks. "Is that what you want right now?"

I nod and swipe the bottle from Julian. When I feel the first hot trickle hit my stomach, the expansion of my insides slows and then comes to a halt. I'm able to suck in a real breath for the first time in

145

what seems like a long while. I take one more fortifying swig before handing it back to Julian.

I can feel their eyes following me, unsure what I'm thinking or planning. Not that I blame them. I imagine my behavior the last minute or so seems kind of strange, if not downright scary. And I have no intention of torturing them even further.

I dig through the backpack until I find my junior high graduation photo and tuck it into my pocket.

"Good luck, Kirby," Julian says.

"Just be yourself," Izzy says.

Feeling weak, but ready, I shoulder the car door open and begin taking the cracked walkway that runs through the front yard. When I make it onto the porch, I glance inside one of the windows and notice a black and orange sign that says "Beware of Ferrets," which I remember from my first visit. It's the only external clue that lets me know this is indeed his sister's place.

Her doorbell is the kind you twist, and when I give it a crank, I can hear an angry set of chimes. I reset my feet on the green Astroturf carpeting, preparing myself. My ears feel hot from the alcohol, attuned to the slightest stirring. Somewhere behind me an airplane is taking off or landing.

I turn the crank again and reset my feet, as if it were somehow vital that they be exactly shoulder-width apart.

Nothing happens.

I turn to look back at the Roadrunner parked across the street. Izzy's and Julian's faces are pressed against the windows, peering through the muddy glass. I shrug my shoulders. Neither of them responds.

This time I knock on the door. Four authoritative raps. I don't hear anything from inside, yet I have an unshakeable feeling Bradley's here. Maybe he's asleep, or he's got headphones on, or he's just wary of whoever might be knocking on the door in the middle of the afternoon.

Cromley

I glance at the neighbor's house, a shoebox similar to this one, but with plywood werewolf and Dracula and witch ornaments impaled in the front yard. Halloween must be right around the corner and I didn't even realize it. Incredible! Somehow this once-critical holiday, whose date I used to circle on my calendar months in advance (dreaming of candy-filled pillow cases and sugar-induced comas), has become as inconsequential as Arbor Day. For the life of me, I can't even remember the last good Halloween I had.

Out of the corner of my eye, I catch a blur of a face disappearing from the neighbor's window and a curtain falling back into place. I've got to stay focused on the business at hand.

"Bradley, are you there?" I say to Edina's door. Three more crisp knocks. "It's me, Kirby Russo," I add, as if the last name might help him place the first a little easier.

There's an ambulance howling somewhere a couple blocks away, a pickup truck with a lousy muffler down the street, and nothing from the other side of the door.

"Please, Bradley." I allow a quavery sadness into my voice in the hope it might make me harder to resist. "I just want to talk with you. Come on and open the door. I've got a message from Debbie." I'm hoping this might be the bait that draws him out of his hermitage.

"She wants to work things out, but she's too embarrassed to drive here and do it herself. She wants you to come home and everything can go back to normal. It's time to bring this family back together. That's all any of us really wants is to just have things the way they were. Sure there were problems, but that's what life is like, no matter where you are or who you're with. And maybe this separation is actually a good thing, and now when we're back home we'll all be a little wiser and we won't have to fall into the same ruts of not appreciating each other. Maybe this time—"

"Kirby."

It's Izzy. She and Julian are standing next to each other on the front walk, hands in their pockets to keep warm. Julian's a good six inches shorter than Izzy and for a second it looks like she might be his mother. It's impossible to tell how long they've been there, how much they've heard.

"Maybe no one's home," she says.

"I really think he is."

"But if he's not answering..."

"I don't know why he's not answering. I only know we didn't come this far to turn around because *someone won't open the goddamn door!*" I'm shouting now, so Bradley can hopefully hear me and get the picture that he can't keep hiding.

"What are you going to do?"

"Simple," I say, taking all three porch steps in one stride. "If he won't come to me, I'll go to him."

I begin tramping around the side of the house. The alcohol's coursing through my bloodstream, making me lightheaded, fearless. In the far corner of the backyard there's a chicken-wire enclosure the size of a station wagon. A skinny, brown-furred ferret with a white bandit mask freezes and looks up at me in surprise when I round the corner, as if I'd caught him in the middle of a clever theft. Once he gets over his initial shock, he stands on his back legs and begins making a muffled barking noise that sounds like, "Chuck-chuck-chuck-chuck."

The screen door is unlocked. I pull it open and knock hard.

"Bradley, did you hear what I said? I'm not going home until we talk. There's no point hiding. I'm not going to do anything but talk. If you're in some kind of trouble we can work that out too."

Three more ferrets have emerged from a plastic hutch in their enclosure. Like their colleague, they have assumed a stance on their hind legs. And they join him in muffled barking. "Chuck-chuck-chuck-chuck-chuck." The four of them standing there look like they're praying.

"Kirby, come on." Izzy and Julian have followed me around the house. "You're making a ton of noise."

Cromley

I'm banging on the door now, which I only realize because my knuckles are getting sore.

"I really think he's not home." Izzy's eyes are squinted and the corners of her mouth are curled into a wincing smile, the kind you make when you see someone else stub their toe.

"Chuck-chuck-chuck-chuck-chuck."

"He's just hiding. Probably scared." I stop hammering on the door. "Here. I'll show you. Julian, give me a boost up to that window."

"Chuck-chuck-chuck-chuck."

Julian laces his fingers and I step on, pulling my chin up over the window ledge. Julian's hands are shaky, but they hold.

"Kirby, get down from there." Izzy's pity is quickly morphing into anger.

"Chuck-chuck-chuck-chuck-chuck-chuck."

The curtain is drawn tight so I can't really see much. Still, I use this new position to project my voice inside.

"Bradley, I know you're in there. I'm not going away until we talk. So come on out."

"Kirby," Izzy shouts, "get down!"

"Chuck-chuck-chuck-chuck."

"Bradley, please. Please come out and we'll go home, please."

"Chuck-chuck-chuck-chuck-chuck-chuck-chuck!"

"That'll be quite enough." It's a different voice this time – not Izzy. "I will thank you for getting down from there this instant, young man."

I turn to see a woman in a green pantsuit standing behind Izzy. She's got a tightly kinked perm that forms a kind of nest for her face, which, from what I can tell, is arranged in a fairly angry expression.

"Aunt Edina," I manage to get out, "it's so good to see you."

At this moment, either from exhaustion or panic, Julian's hands give out. I fall away from the house and spill into a heap on the cold dead grass of the backyard. And it's only then that the ferrets go silent.

Chapter 13

Somewhere in the bowels of this house a furnace is pumping out a stream of hot air infused with the acrid scent of well-used kitty litter. The color palette of her interior décor ranges from brown to rusted orange. A clock ticking in the dining room is insistently reminding me of every passing second. I can feel something – which I hope is a ferret – crawling around the guts of the couch I'm sitting on.

Edina leans against the wooden TV cabinet. "So, Kirby, to what do I owe the honor of your presence?" Her green pantsuit is sucked tight around her butt and thighs, testing the tensile strength of the stitching.

"It's so rare that I get the chance to visit family anymore."

Three years ago, I remember sensing an inexpressible unease around Bradley's sister. Now that I'm back, a little wiser, it's easier to see why. Imagine an infant's entire future life as a vast decision tree, with all the possible permutations mapped out before her. Now, exclude all the horrifically bad decisions, like committing murder or chugging a glass of strychnine. Then, get rid of all the paths that lead to something anyone might consider remotely interesting or noteworthy. The adult Edina is, to me, the worst possible result of the remaining choices – kind of an apotheosis of sub-mediocrity.

The Last Good Halloween

Don't get me wrong – I don't mean this as an insult. I have no idea what factors or forces pushed her to this particular life branch. I'm just saying if there was any way for me to avoid it, I'd sacrifice important body parts to do so.

"Family..." she says, curling her lip in mild disgust. "That's one word for it."

Julian's sitting on the other end of the couch. Izzy's perched on an armchair in the corner, her back straight as if she were sitting for a portrait.

I have no idea what Edina remembers of me from the last time we visited, but in case it's not a fond memory, a little flattery might be the perfect antidote. "You look lovely today, Aunt Edina."

She elaborately rolls her eyes, and in the process reveals a thick application of green eye shadow that matches her pantsuit. There's a certain sexual desperation in the way that emerald smudge is caked on, and I find it oddly alluring, though as soon as that thought passes through my brain, I hate myself for thinking it.

"What do you want, Kirby? Does your mother have any idea where you are?"

Finding it difficult to answer both questions at the same time, I respond to one she didn't ask. "She's doing very well, thank you."

Something furry scampers from behind the TV cabinet to a vinyl beanbag. Izzy, seeing this, crosses her feet nervously.

"If you want, I'll start with the obvious," Edina says, tossing a hand in the air. "Why were you trying to break into my house?"

"A quick review of the evidence will show I was doing no such thing."

She swings her ample hip away from the TV cabinet and cocks it to the other side. It's thick and meaty and encased tightly in her pants fabric. Again I feel a ripple of repressed, hungry desire gnawing embarrassingly at my groin.

"Then what were you doing?" she asks.

"I'd call it aggressively seeing if anyone was home."

Cromley

"And who were you hoping to find at home? *My* home."

"Aunt Edina, I think we both know the answer to that question." I give her a kind of flirty smile, hoping, I guess, to be charming.

"I suppose we do, Kirby." She bends down to the beanbag near her feet. Her slacks make an alarming stretching sound, but they don't give. When she stands back up, she's holding a ferret by the scruff of the neck. This one is white, with pink eyes and ears, and it dangles from her fist like a wet sock.

She lays the ferret in the crook of her arm and rocks it against the pillow of her breast. "Shh-shh-shh-shh," she says to the ferret. "There, there, Angel-Cakes. Just sleepy-bye."

"So," I say, lowering my voice for the sake of Angel-Cakes, "may I speak with him please?"

Her eyes flicker for a second and then quickly deaden. "Who are you talking about?" She asks this as if we hadn't just agreed on the matter a moment ago.

I had no idea she'd drag it out this far, and on some level I have to admire her willingness to be a pain in my ass. As our eyes spar from opposite sides of the room, I remember something from the time we visited her three years ago. After she'd claimed her cookies were homemade, and after I found the wrappers for them in her garbage can, in a fit of youthful rebellion, I removed the packages from the bin, brushed off the coffee grounds and carrot peels, and set them neatly on her kitchen counter. Chips Ahoy! and some kind of generic sugar cookies – side-by-side, soggy, smelly – I left them sitting there. It occurs to me that this game she's playing now might be my payback for that little stunt.

"Aunt Edina," I say, adopting a formal tone, "may I please speak with my father, Bradley Kellogg?"

She smiles and makes a laughing sound in the back of her throat. Julian shifts uncomfortably on the sofa next to me. Izzy uncrosses her legs.

The Last Good Halloween

"Pretty please," I add, since she's already brought me to my rhetorical knees. "With sugar on top. And a cherry."

She keeps smiling. "Nope," she says. "And he's not your father."

"Oh come on!" Izzy erupts as if she's been holding her breath for a long time. "Just let Kirby talk to him!"

Edina sets the sleeping Angel-Cakes on the bean bag. "I can't," she says calmly. "He's not here."

I can sense both Izzy's and Julian's gazes shift onto me. At the same time I get this weird falling sensation in my stomach, as if I'd been standing on ground that's suddenly no longer there.

"Of course he is," I insist. "You don't have to protect him."

"Why on earth would you think he's here?"

"Because the letter he sent to Debbie was postmarked from Great Falls." Saying it, actually hearing the words spoken out loud, I now see how flimsy this evidence is.

"Oh my," she says, chuckling. "Oh my goodness. I can only imagine how embarrassed you must feel right now."

There's more stirring somewhere inside the couch and then a set of whiskers tickling my ankle.

"How do you explain the postmark?" I ask, but my position is feeling less secure with every second that passes.

"He *was* here." She stops chuckling and looks around the room. "He visited a couple weeks ago. It's possible he posted a letter then." She turns and starts walking toward the kitchen. "On some level, I do feel bad you came all this way for nothing."

"Then tell me where he is now."

She hesitates for a moment but doesn't turn around. "I don't think that's a good idea, Kirby. It's best if you go back to Billings and move on."

She enters the kitchen, and a moment later she emerges with a bowl full of kibbles, which she swirls for a few seconds then sets on the floor. The ferret that's been rummaging around in the couch darts out from underneath. Angel-Cakes wakes up and is joined at the food bowl by still more ferrets from parts unknown. In all the times I planned this trip I never once foresaw it turning out like this.

Edina stands up, looking surprised to see we're still in her living room. "Drive safe," she says. "I heard on the radio we might be getting some weather coming in."

"Edina, I'm sorry about the cookie packages. But this is extremely important. I have reason to believe Bradley might be in some kind of trouble."

Her expression doesn't change, not a twitch nor a tic. "I know he is," she says, "but the kind of trouble he's in you certainly can't help him with."

"Where is my stepfather?" I ask, trying to sound like I'm done messing around.

"Bradley's got a lot to sort out," she says flatly

"So do I."

"He's trying to find himself."

"The man is thirty-seven years old," I say. "It seems a little late for that, if you ask me."

Edina takes a small step back from the food bowl, and I realize at some point in the last few minutes I've stood up from the couch.

"Listen," I say, lowering my voice for a different approach, "I understand if he's trying to find himself. That's cool. But maybe by having a conversation with someone who's lived with him for a while, someone who really knows him, we all might be happier with who Bradley ends up finding."

Edina casts a glance at the feasting ferrets. When she looks back at me, I can see a coldness in her eyes that's almost frightening. "Do you honestly not know how difficult you made his life, Kirby?"

My mouth gropes for some words to push out, but they're not there.

"I never liked you. Nor your mother. You're both toxic people, and I hold you two personally responsible for what my brother's become. Even if I did like you, even if you'd never taken those cookie packages out of my goddamn garbage can, I wouldn't tell you where my brother is. I owe him that much."

Izzy and Julian have heard enough. Or maybe they've decided I've heard enough. They've both stood up and moved to my flanks – over-protective bodyguards, ready to hustle me out of harm's way.

"You're breaking up a family here," I say, feeling a sting in the back of my throat. "I hope you know that. I hope that makes you happy."

"That's not what I'd call what you had." She's smiling, but it's an expression that implies a level of distaste. "That was no family."

Apparently, I tried to take a step toward her because Izzy and Julian have grabbed me by the forearms – not gently – and they're now steering me toward the front door.

"Please tell me where he is," I say. By now I have to twist my neck to see her because they've already got me halfway out the door. "You wouldn't believe how happy we were. How happy we could still be!"

They've got me outside now, down the porch steps. Edina is standing in the doorway, arms crossed.

We're almost to the street when all of a sudden I do a windmill thing with my arms and break free of Izzy and Julian. I run back to the foot of the porch and look up at Edina, who's swung the door half-closed at my approach. I know this is my last chance, my last opportunity to explain how important this is, to pluck my heart out of my chest and show it to her as proof that, yes, I am putting everything on the line in order to repair the family that's fallen apart. My pulse is pounding, and the air around me is vibrating. This is exactly how I felt that morning when I hit the accelerator and very nearly ran down Jason Cipriano.

I look up at Edina, I open my mouth, and I say:

"Why don't you go fuck yourself, you viperous cunt! I will take napalm to this shithole!"

Cromley

Before I can measure how effective this approach is, two sets of hands clamp onto my shoulders and begin dragging me back to the Roadrunner, kicking and writhing.

Chapter 14

The diner we're in has one booth at the back and that's where we are. I don't recall seeing the name of the place, nor am I entirely sure how we got here. The last thing I remember was moisture on my cheeks as they stuffed me into the car, and now that I can feel the stiff, salty tracks running down my face I realize it must have been tears.

I wonder what Izzy thought about seeing me cry – if this gratuitous display of emotion built me up or tore me down in her eyes. I suppose it would depend on the context. Was what happened at Edina's place a crying-level event? On that I'm a little fuzzy.

The walls are cluttered with old photographs from various historical periods of Great Falls, stiff portraits of ranch hands, the soot-blackened faces of smelter workers, oversaturated images of 1970s industrial progress. The only other patrons in the place are seated at the counter, their asses spilling over the edges of their mushroom-shaped stools. They're all baseball-capped and wearing some combination of denim, canvas and brown leather.

A clock above the grill shows 3:45, and I have no reason to doubt its accuracy. In a different universe, one where my plan worked, we're streaking back to Billings, followed closely by my stepfather who's preparing to banish Uncle Harley – by force if necessary – and reclaim his seat at the throne of our humble castle. But that's not happening. Slowly, piece by piece, my plan has fallen apart. It's now officially ruined. This realization opens up in me an emptiness so deep and intense it feels like an emotional black hole – not even a glimmer of hope can escape its gravitational pull.

Julian's just started working on a heaping plate of cheese fries. He has a paper napkin fastidiously tucked into his shirt and he's using a knife and fork. Izzy's got a coffee steaming on the table. She's hunched over the letter I intercepted from Bradley, studying it intensely. Like so much that's happened since we left Edina's house, I don't know how Izzy ended up with it. Did I give it to her? Or did she find it on her own? My initial instinct is to snatch it away from her, but there's no telling how long she's been poring over it, so there's probably not much dignity to protect, nor would I even know, at this point, whose dignity I'd be protecting.

"So you really based this whole thing on a postmark." It's not a question, more a confirmation of something she doesn't want to believe.

Julian is methodically spearing his goop-covered fries and popping them into his mouth. It looks disgusting, and probably tastes delicious. I'd take some if I had even the slightest appetite. But I don't.

"I had a hunch too," I say, mustering a feeble defense.

Izzy sets the letter on the tabletop, takes a sip of coffee. "A hunch implies you had some other clue." Her voice sounds brittle. "Some *thing* to make you have the hunch."

"I told you half the envelope got burnt. So I guess the clue was the postmark."

"Exactly." She sets her cup down carefully, in a way that indicates she's tapping into her emergency reserves of patience. "You had a hunch based on a postmark. So, as I said a moment ago, the whole thing was based on a postmark."

Cromley

Julian's still working on his fries, oblivious to the underlying tension. A waitress comes by with a carafe of coffee. I turn my cup over, mostly so I'll have something to do with my hands.

"In theory it was a good plan," I say once the waitress has moved on. "If I would've been right about Bradley being here, we might've pulled it off."

Izzy exhales slowly and looks out the front window. The afternoon light is smudged gray, fast on its way toward dusk. "What happens now?" she asks. "According to your plan?"

I pull out my piece of paper and read off the last three items on it: *No. 10: Drive back to Billings*; *No. 11: Drop off Roadrunner*; *No. 12: Appreciate the restoration of my old life more than I used to.*

"That's why I hate plans," she says coldly. "They never work out."

"This one sure as hell didn't." I toss it onto the table and it knocks over one of the plastic creamer cartons. A slow-moving rivulet of half-and-half starts wending its way across the table toward the letter from Bradley. Izzy rescues the letter but not before the bottom of it gets wet. She blots at it with a paper napkin.

"Should we go?" I say to no one in particular.

"Hey, I'm still eating here." Julian's plate is three quarters empty. He's got some cheese goo that needs to be napkinned off his face.

Izzy's still looking at the letter. Something's caught her attention. She turns it over and holds it closer, as if she's forgotten her reading glasses. Her eyes are scanning feverishly. When she finally looks at me, something in her face has changed.

"How carefully did you look at this?"

I shrug my shoulders. "Pretty carefully."

"You know, I hesitate to even point this out—" she stops, catches herself. "Go ask that waitress for a pencil."

"What?"

"Just do it."

The Last Good Halloween

I slide out of the booth and approach the counter. The waitress gives me an exhausted look, but she eventually relents and pulls a heavily-chewed Dixon Ticonderoga from her apron pocket.

When I give the pencil to Izzy, she scoots down the bench so she's sitting next to me, our thighs parallel, almost touching. "Watch this," she says.

Her face is inches from mine; the last time we were this close was when we kissed in Prospect Park. Under the harsh scrutiny of the overhead lights, I can see a spray of sand-colored freckles that follows the ridge of her cheekbones.

She lays the letter facedown on the tabletop and begins rubbing the flat edge of the pencil lead across one spot. At first it just looks like a grayish wash, but slowly, glyph-like shapes begin to show through. She presses down a little harder and as the graphite darkens, the lettering emerges more clearly.

"He filled out the envelope after he sealed it," Izzy says. "Get it?"

On the back of the letter, in Bradley's unmistakable hand, is the perfect negative image of the return address, which I accidentally destroyed the day I opened the envelope.

BRADLEY KELLOGG
C/O UPTOWN MOTEL
376 WOODY ST.
MISSOULA, MT 59806

"I can't believe that actually works," Julian says through a mouthful of potato and cheese product.

It's so obvious. I mean, I'm sure there's at least a dozen Hardy Boys and Encyclopedia Brown mysteries where they use that exact technique to solve the crime. But also obvious because of the sound of it. *Uptown Motel* conjures images of a rundown flophouse where damaged people might take refuge, lay low, seek answers. *This* is the kind of place Bradley would go to find himself during his emotional standing eight-count. Not his dumb, boring sister's house.

Izzy is watching these thoughts travel across my face, like I'm an actor in a silent movie.

"What do you think?" she asks.

When words finally come to me, they don't make a lot of sense. "I mean... it's so... Missoula."

"He must have written the letter while he was there," she says, "then dropped it in the mail when he was visiting his sister here."

"We were just in Missoula for computer camp," Julian says. "He might've even been there while we were."

"It's a decent chance he's still there," Izzy says. "I mean, who puts a motel as their return address unless they're spending significant time there?" A note of optimism has crept into her voice, and now it hangs over the table between us like a spirit she's called up from a séance.

The only problem is, optimism is the last thing we should be generating right now. I'm not sure how far it is from here to Missoula. I only know that getting there would surely take us late into the night. We probably wouldn't be able to find Bradley 'til tomorrow morning, which would mean we'd maybe start for Billings around noon, which would put us back there tomorrow afternoon – almost twenty-four hours later than the original plan. I can't even begin to imagine the types of contorted excuses we'd need to come up with in order to make it fly. Besides, going to Missoula would present a new set of opportunities for getting arrested, since it's still likely the police are searching for an auto-erotic sex fugitive last seen driving a stolen Roadrunner. Sure, we've covered it in dust and switched the plates, but how long is that ruse realistically going to last?

"We can't go," I say.

"Why not?" Izzy asks.

The Last Good Halloween

"We had a plan. I see now that it was too optimistic. And I'm not going to make that mistake again."

Izzy shrugs. Julian just stares at me.

"Listen," I tell them, "we gave it our best shot and it didn't work out. If we go back home now, there's a chance we won't get caught. Or if we do, we might not get into too much trouble."

Izzy sets her hand on the table. Her sleeve is riding up and for the first time on this trip I can see her Mr. Yuk tattoo, glowing like the face of an alarm clock against the pale skin of her forearm.

"It's up to you and Julian," she says. "I've got nothing to go back to, so it's all the same to me. But you guys, you know, have things to consider."

"It's nice to think about," I say, "but Missoula was never part of the plan."

It's quiet at the table for a moment.

"Let's just settle up the bill and go home."

The spirit of optimism that was here a moment ago has been banished to whatever nether region those things go to when they're not wanted. There's the clinking of silverware from the patrons at the counter. I can hear a low hum coming from the lights overhead. A truck rumbles by on the street outside.

Julian is nearly finished with his fries, leaving only a pool of congealing yellow cheese. He sets his fork like a ramp leading from the tabletop to his empty plate. Then he clears his throat. "How do you make God laugh?" he asks.

"I'm not interested in Christian talk right now, Julian."

"Answer the question," he says. "How do you make God laugh?"

"I have no idea," I say.

"Make a plan," he says, then pauses for a moment to let it sink in. "That's it: Make. A. Plan." This time he punctuates each word with a finger jabbed at the air

Izzy laughs – a little more than you would if you were just being polite.

Cromley

I, however, am less amused. "What's your point, Julian?"

He removes the napkin from his shirt and wads it up. "My point is: Fuck your plan, Kirby."

"Yeah," Izzy says, "screw your goddamn plan!"

A couple of the counter patrons turn their heads in our direction and glare across the diner at us. Izzy waves at them, then turns to me. "What do you say, Ahab? Are you ready to keep chasing that white whale?"

"I've seen the movie version of *Moby Dick*," I tell her. "So I actually get that reference."

She smiles and leans in expectantly.

"If memory serves me correctly, things didn't turn out so great for Ahab."

"Don't you get it, Kirby?" she says. "You have a chance to see this thing through to the end, to finish what you started."

I look across the table at Julian. "Do you really think we should keep going to Missoula?"

A troubled look crosses his face, a tiny flicker of doubt.

"You know what that would mean," I tell him.

"I'm not saying we should go," he admits. "It's a bad idea that probably won't work out." He looks down and rests his fingertips on the table. "But I'm also saying I couldn't stop you if that's what you decided."

I lean back against the cool Naugahyde booth. Julian and Izzy are waiting for me, neither saying a word.

"I'm talking about punishments so big you probably can't even begin to imagine them."

I look from Izzy's face to Julian's. Neither of them seems to be registering an objection. I'm the only one holding us back.

"I'm just saying, you know, in the interest of full disclosure. So you can't say I didn't warn you."

As we sit there in the diner – silence mounting, decision pending, tension ratcheting – my stomach lets out a monstrous

The Last Good Halloween

growl, a profound gurgle that's audible to all three of us at the table. And for the first time today, it feels like I might be able to eat.

Chapter 15

We're on the outskirts of Great Falls, huddled around a payphone. The bar next door is called The Fourth Horseman, and it seems to be doing a brisk business, judging from the number of pickups and motorcycles coming and going in the parking lot. It's dark now and the air has taken on a strange, indecisive feel. Short gusts of wind rip past us, then whirl around and whip the opposite direction.

"When they pick up, tell them we've been hanging out at my house," I advise. "Ask if you can spend the night."

Julian nods tightly. He's holding the receiver cocked so Izzy and I can listen in. His face looks blue in the feeble sputter of the neon beer signs.

Julian and I agreed at the diner that we at least had to try covering our tracks. So we figured we'd use the old sleepover double-switch scam. We did paper-rock-scissors best of seven (I won in five tosses) and that's why he's calling first.

He feeds a couple quarters into the slot and the internal chutes and pathways clink to life. He looks up at me, suddenly panicked. "Should we have an abort code?" he asks.

But it's too late. The line is ringing.

"Hello?" Julian visibly wilts when he hears his mother's voice. "Hello? Who is this? Julian, is that you?"

The Last Good Halloween

Her hoarse urgency is noticeable even through two hundred plus miles of phone line. My heart drops. This is not the sound of a blissfully ignorant parental unit who's about to be snookered by her son and his friends. This is raw maternal panic. It's clear that, while she may not be wise to the entire web we've woven, she's already found enough loose threads to know that something's wrong. And it'll only be a matter of time before the whole scheme unknits.

"It's me, mom." Julian's voice sounds small, childlike. "Everything's fine. I've been hanging out with Kirby and we were—"

"Kirby's mom called an hour ago looking for him."

Next door, a motorcycle starts up and belches thunder before pulling out of the lot, momentarily eclipsing their conversation.

"Where are you, Julian?"

His face seizes into a pained smile. His lips start to flutter. Then he catches himself and slaps a hand over the mouthpiece. "What should I say?"

Izzy shrugs. Her interest in this is purely academic.

"Don't tell her where you are," I say. "Try and see how much she knows."

Resigned to his fate, he uncaps the mouthpiece. "I'm okay, mom. You and dad don't need to—"

"Who were you talking to?" The words are staccato bullets of suspicion.

Julian gulps helplessly at the air. I feel bad he's the one making this call. He's woefully unprepared for it, like in those Vietnam movies when they send the FNG right into the shit.

"Everything's fine, mom."

"Your voice sounds strange, Julian. You still haven't told me where you are."

"I can't tell you right now. It's complicated."

"Is someone stopping you?" Then, chilled by the prospect of her own suggestion, Mrs. Miller lets out an agonized shriek.

Cromley

Julian looks at me, eyes pleading like an actor who's forgotten his lines. I've got nothing for him.

"Julian, I want you to tell me where you are right now." Mr. Miller has taken over the phone line. He barks his words like a man who's used to having his orders followed.

"Dad—"

"Listen to me, son. If you can't tell me where you are because someone's stopping you, say the word *seatbelt*."

"Dad, I'm not—"

"Just say the word *seatbelt*, Julian. Are you listening to me? Listen to me."

And that's when Julian's eyes go haywire – widening and darting like an antic cartoon character. He presses a finger to his temple as if to slow his brain down. Something is brewing deep inside this kid, some pressure is building, looking for an escape valve. Sensing the approach of a dangerous stream of invective, and worried that it might give away our location or otherwise further incriminate us, I reach out and press down on the metal hang-up bar.

"No!" Julian yells, oblivious to the fact that no one's on the other end of the line anymore. "Listen, listen, listen to me! If you would for once in your life shut your fat mouth and listen to me, you'd hear I'm not saying *seatbelt*! But you don't listen, do you? No, you only talk. You only tell people what to do. What I hate about you is every single second your mouth is open I can smell that horrible Listerine breath that's covering up the coffee you drink and the tobacco you chew. It stinks, dad. It reeks."

Julian gulps in another lungful of air. "I'm done listening to you. All right? No more. For once, you can listen to me!"

He seems to have worn himself out because he drops the receiver and it dangles from its metal cable. Some of the Fourth Horseman patrons have stopped to take in the performance. As the three of us stand there looking at each other, I can't help but feel a measure of pride at who Julian's turning out to be.

The Last Good Halloween

"I'm sorry I hung up before you got to say that," I tell him.

"It's all right," he says.

A few tiny snowflakes drift down, pushed in odd, unpredictable swirls by the gusting wind.

"That maybe would have been good for your dad to hear."

"I think most important was getting it off my chest."

Izzy retrieves the receiver and hangs it up. "Personal growth aside, you guys realize his parents now probably think he was kidnapped. Most likely by Kirby."

This sinks in for a moment.

Julian says, "Wow."

Izzy says, "Wow is right."

Then, for some reason, I start to laugh. It's not happy, or joyful necessarily. It's the kind of laugh you might do if you were so completely tired and beaten that you didn't feel like you had any other option but *to* laugh.

It must seem pretty odd, because Izzy and Julian just watch me for a minute. At first they think I'm crying, then eventually they get it and start laughing too, in the same slow, almost-injured way as me.

It goes on like this for a few minutes, sustained by some deep reservoir of something that's in all three of us. And whatever that something is – an emotion? a feeling? – it's slowly leaking out of us, dissipating in the now-cold air. When it all seems gone, Julian says:

"I can hardly remember how we got here."

Izzy and I go quiet, trying to go through all the steps that brought the three of us to this exact spot at this exact time. The truth is we can't, and it probably doesn't matter anyway.

Izzy got directions to Missoula from a pony-tailed patron of The Fourth Horseman. He was wearing a pair of coveralls that looked like they'd been issued from either a garage where he worked or a prison he'd broken out of. The patch stitched on his left breast said

Cromley

"Barry" in white letters. At the time we approached him he was stumbling around the parking lot and may well have been casing the joint for a car to boost. It seemed counterintuitive to ask directions from someone who seemed so lost in so many ways. But Barry claimed there were three different routes to Missoula. We told him we wanted the fastest route, and he frowned for a moment in deep thought. When he finally finished giving us directions, we thanked him. He made a pistol with his thumb and forefinger and shot each of us as a way of saying, "You're welcome."

Now – as per Barry's instructions – we're tooling down a narrow highway, periodically slowing as the speed limit dips for every one-stoplight town along the way. Ahead of us the mountains loom. On the other side of those mountains is Bradley. I couldn't begin to tell you where the BRI stands right now, and I'm not sure how much it even matters anymore.

One thing our drunken direction-giver did not or could not foresee was that those few flakes we saw in Great Falls have steadily amassed allies and are now what I would officially label a snowstorm. Other drivers must have known this was coming, because we're the only car on the road.

Julian is stretched out across the backseat with his jacket covering him like a blanket. The trauma of the conversation with his parents and his subsequent emotional venting have left him drained. He hasn't made a sound in a while and is likely out cold. Izzy's riding shotgun. She's got the roadmap spread across her lap, though it's too dark to read it.

The flakes are fat and heavy. Caught in the high beams, they seem to be rushing at us, like stars when a rocket ship blasts into hyper- or warp- or whatever-drive.

"Kinda mesmerizing, huh?" Izzy says.

I wasn't asleep but definitely in a mental fugue state and it takes a second to shake myself out of it. "Yeah," I say, clearing my throat, "I guess so."

The Last Good Halloween

"What were you thinking about just there?"

"Right now I'm thinking how much I hate it when people ask me what I'm thinking." I have no idea why this is the response I give.

"Honestly," she says, "you're the most tightly wound person I know. It's like you're secretly angry at the world."

"I wouldn't say the *entire* world."

Izzy hasn't bothered to find a radio station so the speakers are piping in clouds of static, disrupted occasionally by voices at the very edge of perception that come and go without warning.

"I'm not sure why that is," she says. "I'm working on a theory that it's because your expectations are too high."

A small gust of wind lifts some snow from the blacktop into a smoky specter, which the Roadrunner's grill promptly blasts through.

"It's not really about you individually. It's more of a global theory that you happen to embody. The basic gist is that high expectations are the cause of a significant portion of the world's human misery. If you expect great or even good things to happen in your life, you're bound to be disappointed, and, thus, miserable. On the other hand, if you don't have any expectations, nothing is worse than it should be. And the slightest good thing that comes along is like a gift from the gods."

"Interesting theory," I say. "Could be worth running some clinical trials."

"Trust me, high expectations'll kill you, Kirby. Or at least they'll make life a lot worse than it has to be."

Julian wriggles around in back for a moment, then murmurs something about not wanting to take the garbage out.

"It's not Debbie that's the problem," I say. "It's me. I drove Bradley away."

"What?" Izzy asks, momentarily thrown.

"You asked what I was thinking back there." I flex my fingers against the steering wheel, trying to push fresh blood into the fingertips. "I was remembering one time I got on this fishing kick with Bradley. Every day – *take me fishing, take me fishing, take me fishing*. The guy had never been fishing in his life, right? Finally it must've gotten so bad he broke down and went to Scheel's and got us some fishing gear. Drove us out to Lake Josephine. Neither of us knew what we were doing – stringing line, tying knots – it was a mess. But, lo and behold, on the second try I caught one. An eight-inch, rinky-dink something. Who knows what it was."

Izzy interrupts, "Kirby, you don't have to tell me this. You're letting what your aunt said get to you."

"So this thing is flopping around on my line. I don't even know how to get it off the hook. So what do I do? I tell Bradley I want to keep it. I want to eat it for dinner. Think about it: If he didn't know how to *fish,* he sure as hell didn't know how to *clean* one. But he also knew me enough to know I'd never let up. So he took it into the bushes."

Izzy's hands are gripping the edges of the map. I can tell she doesn't want to hear this story, but I feel duty-bound to keep going, to see this through to the end. I can't stop, can't help myself.

"Bradley had some cheapo pocket knife. And he's in the bushes and I start hearing this swearing. 'Shit!' 'Goddamnit!' 'Motherfucker!' It was the first time I heard an adult openly swearing. And it got to me. I started laughing. At first it was just these little giggles that I could pretend were hiccups. But then they got bigger. I don't even know what was so funny. The poor guy was miserable in the bushes butchering that fish."

A gust of snow-laden wind strikes the car and I have to ease it back into our lane.

"This is not a good use of your mental energy," Izzy says.

I know she's right, but I go on, pulled by some internal, unstoppable momentum.

"After a while, Bradley must have heard me laughing because he tried to muffle it. But it was too late. I couldn't help myself – even though I already, in that moment, felt horrible for it. Eventually, Bradley came out of the bushes and went back to the car to wrap up what was left of the fish. When we got home, Debbie took one look at the mess in that newspaper and threw it out. The fishing equipment went into the basement furnace closet and we never used it again."

It's quiet for a minute, and then, suddenly, the radio clouds part and we can hear the sound of Michael Dukakis talking in his emotionless, robot voice. "I'm not saying we don't have problems. I'm just not sure my opponent has the right solutions to them..." For a few seconds his voice is so clear it sounds like he's right there in the car with us. And then the clouds quickly regather before we can figure out what problems or solutions he's talking about.

"Why did you tell me that story?" Izzy asks.

"The point is, who'd want to be my father? Sure as hell not me."

"That's not what I take away from it."

"Honestly, I'm not even thinking about convincing him to come back to Billings anymore. At this point, the best thing I can do is apologize to the man and wish him a happy life – at least happier than the one I gave him."

"Christ almighty!" Izzy says, balling her fists and bringing them down on the road map. "No more of this pity-party. I hate to disappoint you, but you're not that abnormal."

"I wasn't trying to enter a competition," I say.

The snow is starting to whiten the edges of the road, inching its way in from the shoulders. In the rearview mirror, I can see a pair of distant headlights cutting through the dark. It's the only other car I've noticed since we left the immediate vicinity of Great Falls. And it makes me feel less alone knowing it's back there.

"Let me ask you something." She doesn't say anything for a minute, as if she hasn't yet decided what she's going to ask. "Have you ever wondered how I knew your name at the beginning of the school year?"

Cromley

"I thought about it. I figured you'd seen it on an assignment or something."

"And did you ever wonder who wrote PSYCHO on your locker?"

"What? My locker doesn't say that. It says—"

"TIPSY-CHOICE. That was pretty clever, I have to admit."

Everything is quiet except for the wind outside and the radio static inside. A glance in the rearview mirror lets me know that the car behind us is gaining.

"Izzy, what are you trying to say?"

"Don't get mad." She reaches out and sets a hand on my knee, but not in a flirtatious way. "I was there too," she says, "in Four-North."

Then she picks her hand back up and looks out the passenger window, into the inky blackness and her own half-reflection.

"I don't remember seeing you there." My voice sounds unfamiliar to my own ears. "They made you wear Velcro shoes too?"

"We only overlapped a few days," she says. "I know it's etiquette to mind your own business, but I couldn't help looking around, seeing if I recognized anyone. I was lonely I guess."

"Why did you write PSYCHO on my locker? That was mean."

"After I did it, I felt like an asshole. That's why I never told you. At the time, I thought I was being clever. Maybe I was trying to reach out. I don't really know."

"Do you know what I was in for?"

She shrugs her shoulders.

"Unofficially, it was for attempted vehicular homicide."

She nods as if that makes sense.

"What about you?"

Her hands fidget on top of the map for a few seconds. "I have a habit of cutting myself sometimes. This summer I accidentally took it too far. Passed out and the next thing you know they've got me in Four-North."

The wind shudders the car, and the static kicks up on the radio.

The Last Good Halloween

"I'm glad we know that about each other," I say. "I'll try not to think any differently about you. In case you were worried."

"I wasn't," she says. "Not with you."

That car behind us is close now. I'm starting to ease off the gas in case the guy wants to pass, when a swirl of blue lights comes on and fills the interior of the Roadrunner.

An electric current jolts through me. I'm seized by an almost primordial impulse to gun it – see how fast this jalopy can burn. I will be Bo-Fucking-Duke and that cop will be Roscoe P. Coltrane. And yet, like all impulses not acted upon immediately, this one works its way through me and ebbs, leaving me frazzled, slicked with sweat, acquiescent.

"Were you speeding?" Izzy asks.

"Not even close."

Julian, awake now, shoots upright. "What's going on?"

"This is it, Julian." I'm easing over to the shoulder, though it's hard to tell where it is due to all the snow that's built up. "We gave it a good run."

Once we've stopped, the cop car pulls around us and parks at an angle so it's blocking both lanes ahead.

"That seems a little excessive," Izzy says.

"He probably wants to wait for backup," Julian says.

"Does he really think he'll need it?"

The car door swings open and a trooper climbs out. He's wearing one of those Mountie hats and a long duster coat. Other than my mom's ex-boyfriend Ray, I have exactly zero experience talking with cops. Though my general sense is that a demeanor of tail-wagging subservience is the most likely way to limit the damage in these types of situations.

My hands feel like they belong to someone else and it's a struggle to get my window rolled down. The air that slips in through the opening is colder than I'd expected. It hits the layer of sweat that's broken out across my skin and raises a set of feverish chills.

Cromley

The trooper reaches the window, then glances back at the road behind us. He bends at the waist and lays his forearm across the car roof. He takes a long, slow look around the inside of the car, from me, to Izzy, to Julian.

"Is there a problem, officer?" I ask sweetly.

"What in Sam Hill're you trying to prove?"

"Well, sir," I start, "I'm, um... It's really simple ... We... just..."

Izzy leans over to rescue me. "Sir, it's very important that my friend here talks to his stepfather in Missoula."

The trooper stands motionless for a moment as if the power of his glare alone might somehow induce shame. "Haven't you ever heard of a telephone?" he says at last.

"Officer, if you only knew how important it is—"

"There is no way on earth *this* car should be driving on *this* road in *this* kind of weather."

All I can do is stare at the trooper and blink.

"You ain't gonna make it through Rogers Pass," he says. "Weather's only getting worse. DOT's shutting it down."

"Then what're we supposed to do?" Izzy asks, a little more pugnaciously than I would have liked, considering it now seems apparent that we perhaps have *not* been caught red-handed as kidnapping sex criminals in a stolen car.

"You can't keep going the way you're going," he says, almost philosophically, as if he weren't talking about driving at all. "You'll have to take another route. There's at least two other ways to Missoula."

"We need to get there tonight," she insists.

The trooper takes a half-step back. "If you proceed any further on this road, I will arrest you and impound your vehicle." He pauses to let this sink in. "Is that understood?"

"Yes, officer," I say, before Izzy can get another word out. "We'll turn around right away." And then I roll my window up.

The Last Good Halloween

His message relayed, the trooper goes back to his own car. He pops the trunk and pulls out some traffic flares, which he ignites and begins placing at regular intervals across the road. The fat flakes of snow, turned pale pink in the burning lights, look very nearly beautiful.

"We can't stay in a motel," Izzy says.

"I've got cash," I say. "Enough to get a room."

She shakes her head. "Motels are the first place the cops send descriptions of people they're looking for."

We're heading back toward Great Falls. The snow has gotten worse in the last few minutes so that now I'm barely going 35 and even that feels like a risk.

"If they're looking so hard for us, why didn't that trooper do anything?" Julian asks.

"Highway Patrol must be on a different cop network," she says. "Or else he was too worried about closing the road to pay attention. Either way, we got lucky. If we go to a motel, even the seediest one in Great Falls, they're going to want to see IDs and a license plate number. So that's out."

"What should we do?" I ask, because, for once, I'm inclined to agree with her.

Izzy studies the map in the meager ambient light. "We could take the long way around – go there via Helena. That'd mean backtracking a good hour or so beforehand. In this weather. Which'd put us into Missoula – I don't know – really late."

"Or?" Julian asks, because the way she said it seemed to hint at another option.

"Well, we could pull off in one of the towns along the road here. Maybe sleep in the car 'til morning. The pass might be clear by then."

"So two options," I say.

"Basically, yeah."

Cromley

"How should we do this?"

"We should put it to a vote," Julian says.

"How democratic," I say.

Izzy sighs heavily and looks out her window, but does not disagree.

Chapter 16

By the time Izzy tells me to hang a right, we're trudging through whiteout conditions, and turning the wheel has become an act of pure faith. But I do as she says, set my jaw, and prepare for whatever impact lies ahead.

"According to the map, the name of this town is Simms," Izzy says.

It turns out she was being uncharacteristically charitable. Simms is less like a town and more like a cluster of mobile homes planted amid a maze of dirt roads.

"We're going to freeze to death," Julian says.

"Maybe you should've thought of that before you voted to spend the night in the car," Izzy says. "You've lost the right to bitch."

"We'll turn the engine on and run the heat every once in a while so we don't run out of gas," I say. I also voted to spend the night in the car, though that was only because I'm about to pass out from tiredness.

Once I've found a spot in the dirt road maze that seems suitably dark and inconspicuous, I pull the car to a halt. As soon as I turn the engine off and the cold begins to seep in through the vents and window gasketry, I catch myself wishing I'd had the foresight to at least pack a blanket or sleeping bag.

The Last Good Halloween

"I'm already cold," Julian says from the backseat.

No one responds. I can sense the effort Izzy's exerting to not snap at him.

"You know," he goes on, "this is how people die. Seriously. Hypothermia. I read about this exact thing. These people got lost on this old logging road. So they decided to spend the night in the car because it seemed like the warmest place."

"Quit jabbering back there," Izzy says.

"Later that night they got real peaceful," he says. "And then they just fell asleep and didn't wake up. Froze to death. Human popsicles. No one found the bodies 'til spring."

I reach for the ignition and Izzy says, "You turn on the heat now and he'll find something else to complain about."

She's right. It's clear Julian's starting to lose it. My guess is that it's a delayed reaction to the situation he's found himself in with his parents. The first serious trouble he's ever gotten into. PTSD for someone who's never actually done anything to warrant it. Still, if I don't try something, he's liable to fly off into a full-on, teeth-gnashing freak-out.

I turn the engine over and let the heat flow back through the vents. As soon as Julian feels it, he begins to settle back down, slipping toward the depths of slumber he'd been trolling before the trooper pulled us over.

"Maybe you were wrong," I say.

Izzy shrugs and wraps her arms tighter around herself.

"I'll turn it off when he falls asleep."

Even as the words disperse into the damp interior, I can feel the heat getting to me. My eyelids grow heavy. They sag further and further until they're closed. I keep expecting Izzy to say something, to wake me up, but she doesn't, and I realize she must be nearly asleep as well. My brain starts to spin down, playing its own personal national anthem before ending its broadcast day and cutting over to color bars. For a second, I remember something about needing to turn off the car, yet there's no way to physically lift my hand right now – it's simply too heavy.

Just when my fade seems so total and complete as to be irreversible, I become dimly aware of a distant sound. It's quiet and muffled, but, like a bird singing in the pre-dawn hours to a sun he is certain will rise, this sound is not going away.

My brain reluctantly begins to cycle back up toward consciousness. The sound grows clearer. It's a voice. Female. Adult. I pry open my eyes.

There's a light coming from the house we're parked closest to. I know for certain it had been completely dark a few minutes ago, so this can't be a good development. With the jolt of adrenaline this realization provides, I'm able to rouse myself to a level of semi-functionality. I wipe a circle on the foggy window and peer out into the dark and falling snow.

A cone of light illuminating a small wooden porch. A cracked front door with a head poking out of it.

I unroll the window an inch and cock my ear.

"Helloooooo," the head is saying. "Can I help you?"

I roll the window back up and look at my passed-out companions. What would happen if I just went back to sleep? Alternatively, what would happen if I pulled away, tried to drive further down the road?

I look back outside. The porch light is still shining.

"Do you need help?" the voice calls when I unroll the window again.

I stick my head outside. Snowflakes are sifting gently onto my hair. And because it's true and because I don't have much other choice, I cup my hands to my mouth and holler back, "Yes. Yes, we do!"

The living room couch, which Izzy, Julian and I occupy, is on the opposite side of the room from the owners' recliners. If there was a card table between us, we could all easily eat dinner off of it. The house is cram-packed with stuff, yet it doesn't feel cluttered. Everything looks like it's exactly where it belongs – a complex puzzle that miraculously fits together. The place is overwhelmingly equine-themed: horse figurines on the shelves, horse paintings on the walls, horse ashtrays on the coffee tables, horse glasses filled with milk in our hands.

Felix and Mary Adler appear to have some time ago reached that level of elderliness where I cannot safely hazard a guess as to their age. They could be anywhere between sixty and ninety, though part of that might be because I've never really known any older people – neither Debbie's nor Bradley's parents are still alive – so I couldn't tell you *this* is what seventy looks like, or *that* is eighty-five.

Regardless, the Adlers have deep facial crevasses, craggy knuckles, crystalline irises, and hair that seems to be growing and not growing in unlikely places for their respective genders. It's almost like they've evolved, over time, to resemble each other. And as they sit in their brown recliners with matching brocaded lassos on the armrests, it looks as if they might be bookends of some sort.

"My goodness the weather is demonic out there tonight," Mrs. Adler says. She's got those nervous lips that always seem to be moving even when she's not talking.

There's a loose pile of Uno cards on the end table between them.

"Yes," Izzy says, "definitely satanic atmospheric conditions." She's on the far side of the couch with her arms crossed. She hasn't said it, but I can tell she's unhappy about being here. Julian, in the middle, has barely regained consciousness from the car. His head is lolling, eyelids drooping.

"Only a fool'd try and drive through *that*," Mr. Adler snorts. Up until now, he's been preoccupied with monitoring Julian's dips and nods. He has a gruffer manner than his wife, making it plain that he, like Izzy, is not exactly thrilled by our presence. He's got thick Popeye forearms which he has draped over his armrests.

"We weren't paying attention to the weather reports," I say. "Hadn't even planned on going to Missoula 'til this afternoon."

"Missoula," Mr. Adler says with a measure of disgust. "You'd've never made it tonight."

"My husband was a long-haul trucker," Mrs. Adler says with some tenderness. "He knows these roads better than most."

The old man nods his head gravely. He reaches out to straighten the Uno cards and I catch a glimpse of a faded anchor tattoo.

"Between the ages of eighteen and sixty-five," he says, "the majority of the pisses I thrown was in truck-stop bathrooms. You might never think about measuring your life in pisses, but that's the currency of the long hauler." His eyes have gone out of focus in recollection of those many pisses.

"Thing I hated most about it though, the thing I couldn't stand more'n anything, was being away from home." His eyes snap back to the here and now, and they fall heavily on his wife next to him, and it's clear to all of us that *home* is *her*.

"You say you were headed to Missoula?" Mrs. Adler asks, blushing at finding herself the center of attention.

"Yes, ma'am," I say. "I've got family there I was hoping to visit."

"Oh my," she says, "they'll be awfully worried. You ought to call and let them know you're okay. The phone's right there in the kitchen."

Mr. Adler lets out a theatrical sigh at his wife's gesture of charity. She's the generous one, kind to a fault. He reins her in from time to time but is secretly glad she does it.

"I wouldn't want to impose," I say.

"It's really no trouble," she says.

The Last Good Halloween

"Yes, Kirby," Izzy says through her teeth, "you wouldn't want people to worry about us." She's telegraphing something, though I can't discern the message.

Mrs. Adler points me to the kitchen, which is really more of a nook off the living room. The wall phone is avocado green and one of those rotary dial types. I pause for a moment, unsure what number to actually call. Then, without really making up my mind, I start dialing home. I wonder what Debbie will say when she hears from me, if there's any way to convince her I'm all right, how she'll react if I tell her I'm trying to track down Bradley.

As I game plan the conversation in my head, there's no scenario I can envision where it turns out well, so at the last second, instead of a five, I stick my finger in the six socket. The conversation in the living room goes quiet as everyone strains to listen in.

"Hello?" a tired voice on the other end says.

"Hi, it's me," I say.

"Who is this?"

"No, we're okay. We hit some weather on the way to Missoula, so we had to pull over for the night."

"What are you talking about, guy? You got the wrong number."

"We got lucky and this nice couple let us use their phone. We'll sleep in the car 'til tomorrow morning, then push on when the roads are clear."

"Why are you telling me this?"

"I thought you'd want to know," I say.

"Why would I care? Do you have any idea what time it is?"

"We'll see you sometime hopefully mid-morning, okay? And don't worry about us. We'll be fine."

"Who is this? Who are you? Why are you calling?"

"I love you too." Then I hang up.

I'm about to turn back to the others when I catch sight of the dining room through a doorway to my right. A horseshoe chandelier casts a dull glow on a pair of medium-sized pumpkins sitting on the table. They've been carved with some expertise – big, goofy eyes and toothless grins – recently, I would guess, based on the unmistakable smell of freshly extracted pumpkin guts. How strange. The Adlers obviously don't have young children anymore. I wonder what the purpose of these could be.

Then Izzy clears her throat in the living room and I'm pulled away from this mini-mystery for the time being.

"Everything's A-Okay," I say brightly when I've returned.

"Everything is absolutely *not* okay," Mrs. Adler says.

I look at the couch – at Izzy sitting with her arms crossed, at Julian nearly comatose. Did something transpire while my back was turned, some silent signal to make everything not copacetic?

"There is no way I'm going to let three lost souls sleep out in their car on a night like this."

Izzy uncrosses her arms. "That's very generous, Mrs.—"

"Nonsense." She holds up an arthritic forefinger for emphasis. "My husband and I simply will not allow you to sleep in your car. It's un-Christian."

"Really," I say, "it would be wrong to trouble you."

But she re-brandishes her nonsense-halting finger.

"For crying out loud," Mr. Adler says, "Mary, we can't force them to stay. For all they know we could be deranged psychotics."

She shifts her gaze to her husband. "Do we look like deranged psychotics?" she asks.

"The ones who don't look like it are the most dangerous kind," he says.

She shakes her head and makes a tsk-tsk-ing sound with her tongue. "I seem to recall, Mr. Felix Adler, many a time on your hauls when you benefitted from the unforeseen kindness of strangers."

Her eyes bore into him for a few seconds until something in him relents. He reaches over and sets his hand gently on his wife's lasso armrest.

The Last Good Halloween

"She's right." He smiles as he makes this concession, seemingly pleased to have lost the argument. "Let me go fix the camper. It's not going to be an oven, but it'll be warmer than that car. And it's got beds so you might even get a good night's rest."

Mr. Adler rises on creaky knees and a moment later we can hear him go out the back door.

"And your friend's going to be all right?" Mrs. Adler asks, tilting her chin toward Julian.

"He's had a long day," Izzy says. "He'll be good as new once he gets some rest."

As I watch Mrs. Adler nod doubtfully, it occurs to me: These people, this man and woman, possess something hugely important. You can tell just by looking at them – they're happy, content. They enjoy being with each other, even though they spend nearly every waking moment in a tiny, overstuffed trailer home. The Adlers must have stumbled upon some divine algorithm that's unlocked the mysteries of life and happiness. And maybe us finding ourselves here tonight is not just a random occurrence. Maybe the whole point of us ending up here was for me to notice this and discover what the secret is. Because if I can figure it out, I might be able to pass it on to Bradley and Debbie. And it could be the elixir that revives their marriage and restores the home that's fallen into decay.

"You and your husband seem...happy," I say. My voice sounds flighty, keyed up with an excitement I can't control.

"I guess you could say we are," she says.

"Do you mind if I ask how long you've been married?"

"Well, let's see now." Her lips flutter as she does the mental calculations. "I guess forty-nine years now."

"Amazing."

She smiles, but I can tell she's not sure what's so amazing about it.

"And... wow. So genuinely *wonderful*."

"Yes, dear, very wonderful."

Cromley

"What's the secret?" I ask, tossing all caution aside.

The wrinkles across her forehead deepen. "Secret to what?"

"To this." I throw my arms out to encompass her whole tiny house. "All of it."

Mrs. Adler seems genuinely perplexed. "I'm not sure I follow you," she says, though she sounds like she really wishes she could.

"You're both so obviously happy," I say, again trying to pin her down. "You've been married almost fifty years and you seem like you actually enjoy each other's company. You have to admit that's kind of strange, right?"

"I never thought about it that way."

"Trust me, it's not normal. Most couples, if they've even managed to make it that long, can't stand to be in the same room with each other."

She shrugs her shoulders.

"Do those pumpkins in the dining room have anything to do with it?"

"Oh that," she says, seemingly grateful for something concrete to discuss. "That's just a silly ritual we do every Halloween. Even after our kids moved away. Felix still hides eggs on Easter and fills our stockings at Christmas."

"Do you expect me to believe that's your secret?"

She ponders this a moment, lips ablur.

"How on earth have you managed to stay so happy for so long?"

When she finally speaks, she starts off slowly as if she's still not sure of the question. "Why would you worry about how something like that happens?" she says. "It just does."

"That's it?" I ask, crestfallen.

"Everything in life just happens," she says, "as long as you let it."

How completely unsatisfying. How totally, cluelessly naïve.

This is as close as I'm going to get to her secret. She's not lying to me or holding back. I just think she was fortunate enough so that

The Last Good Halloween

in *her* life everything *did* just happen, and it all happened to turn out well. Not all of us were born that lucky.

Chapter 17

The camper smells like an old canvas tent that's been put away wet and left for a long time. It's also cold, but Mr. Adler has stocked it with a generous supply of wool blankets. When he came back to the house he told us the water wasn't running in the camper because of the danger of freezing pipes, so the three of us took turns washing up inside before heading out for the night.

By the time I finish brushing my teeth with my finger and high-stepping it through the snow, Julian is already curled up in a foldout cot near the front of the camper. I suppose if I were more awake right now, I'd be worried about him. The kid has done and seen more today than he has in the previous fifteen years of his life combined. That's bound to take a toll. Then again, I'm not on the surest of emotional footing right now either, so I'm probably not the right guy to talk him through it. For the time being I'll just have to hope he can pull himself out of it on his own. As a precautionary measure, I hold the back of my hand up to his face to make sure he's breathing. Then I carefully pull his blankets to his chin and tuck them in so they don't fall off in the middle of the night.

The camper itself is the size of a luxurious bathroom. Once you get past the front entrance where Julian's cot is, there's basically one room, kind of an all-purpose living/dining room. A pile of extra

The Last Good Halloween

blankets is stacked on the living/dining room bench. To the back is an alcove kitchen. Over that is a loft which contains the only other bed in here. I was not prepared for a situation so highly booby-trapped with potential sexual awkwardness, which could directly lead, if I'm not careful, to sexual humiliation. Izzy's still in the house. I only have a moment to decide how to play this. I'm not sure what the proper or gentlemanly thing to do is. I'm not even sure if they're the same thing in this situation. All I know is I need to make the right call if I'm going to avoid near-certain embarrassment.

Outside, good-nights are being exchanged and the backdoor closes. A few seconds left to make up my mind. Quickly, I toss half the blankets onto the loft. Then I stretch out on the living/dining room bench and cover myself with the remaining ones.

A moment later, a gust of cold air whooshes in along with Izzy. I close my eyes, feigning sleep. Through my tightly pressed eyelids, I sense her standing over Julian, and then, just like I did, she makes sure his covers are secure. I can feel her bodily aura as she comes into the living/dining room.

"Are you asleep?" she whispers.

I murmur and roll over sleepily.

"That was quick," she says.

She climbs up to the loft and lays out the blankets across the mattress. I hear her boots plunk, one, two, onto the floor before she climbs the rest of the way up. For a few minutes, I'm aware of the sounds of her body shedding its wakefulness, a little tossing and turning and then nothing. An uneasy calm settles over the camper. Whatever I was worried about, I think I've avoided it.

I remember how tired I was just a short while ago. My bio-rhythms once again begin to wind down. Then, just as sleep looks like a possibility on the horizon, Izzy says,

"You'd probably sleep better up here." Her voice is matter of fact. She knows I'm awake. There's no point pretending.

"I'm okay," I say.

Cromley

"There's plenty of room. And I'm sure it'd be way more comfortable."

"This bench is surprisingly luxurious."

"It only has to be weird if you make it weird, Kirby."

Unable to argue with her logic and, truthfully, not feeling likely to get a good night's rest on this bench, I rise – keeping my blankets wrapped around me for warmth – and scale the ladder to the loft.

"Isn't that better?" she asks. Her voice is suddenly very close.

It's darker in the loft and I can just make out the features on her face.

"We really got lucky," I say. "With the Adlers."

"What was with that grilling you gave the old lady back there?"

"I was just trying to do some recon."

She shakes her head and laughs richly in the back of her throat.

Then it's quiet between us.

"Well," I say, "we better get some sleep."

"Good night, Kirby."

I don't close my eyes. I can't close my eyes. Izzy is moving inside her blanket shell. Then she's unwrapping herself and her hand is drifting toward my face.

But she doesn't touch me, doesn't make contact. Her hand hovers there in front of my nose and she says,

"Kirby."

My lips won't move. My body feels rigor-mortic. Why am I so terrified?

"Kirby."

"What?"

"This is me you're smelling."

I realize I haven't been breathing. When I finally do inhale, I understand immediately what she's talking about. "Oh my God!"

She says, "I was hoping that would shock you."

The Last Good Halloween

All at once, I can feel the palms of her hands on my chest and her weight is pressing down on me and I can see her face above me framed by the dingy ceiling tiles and her eyes are closed and her upper lip is tucked behind her bottom teeth. There's a loud roaring sound in my ears. My brain is pressing hard against the insides of my skull.

"Are we doing this?" The roaring sound is so loud I can't tell if it's me or her that asks this.

Slowly, she eases herself back so her weight rests on my pelvis. I can breathe again.

"*Should* we?" This time I'm pretty sure it's me who asks this, though I don't know why I would be expressing even the slightest hint of doubt or reservation.

"I won't be around forever, Kirby," she says.

Izzy shifts her weight back and forth. At first, everything is kind of tight and frictiony, but then, without warning, it becomes smooth. It's happening. I'm in contact with some fiery, molten core.

As someone who has devoted hundreds, if not thousands, of hours in contemplation and anticipation of this exact moment, there are a few things I'm noticing that never once made it into any of my mental dry runs. For instance, I'm surprised by how aware I am of the other things around me besides the sex we're having. It's as if my field of awareness has been expanded and amplified to some kind of freakish level. I could tell you there are three horses in the painting on the wall to my left, which looks suspiciously like a paint-by-numbers project. I could peg the ambient room temperature at somewhere between fifty and fifty-five degrees Fahrenheit – or ten to thirteen degrees Celsius. I could pretty accurately recreate the grain pattern on the wood wall paneling above my head, which forms a lightning strike ZZZZZZ pattern. And I could tell you the sheets of this bed are made of some kind of synthetic fabric that's making my skin itch like crazy.

Cromley

Of course, this hyper-sensitivity is not limited to the room around me. I'm aware of how thin Izzy looks. How her hip bones jut out alarmingly, how her ribs look like contour lines on a map, how the recesses above her clavicles appear dark and bottomless. I can feel a crosshatch of scars on her thighs, which she probably gave herself. And I'm aware that she weighs barely anything and I feel like I have to hold onto her so she doesn't fly away or dematerialize.

If you were to judge purely by physical movement, you'd say it's clear she knows more about the act of sexual congress than me. Though I can sense her shivering a little, which I don't think is from the cold, and which makes me feel a little more equal, like she might actually be as nervous about this as me.

I'd like to say it goes on all through the night and that by some fluke of genetic alchemy, I'm a sexual world-beater. But that would be a lie. I'm not entirely sure how long the whole thing lasts, though I know it's not terribly long. And when Izzy realizes I've been done for a while, she collapses in a heap on my chest and then rolls off to the side.

The quiet in the camper feels like a malicious force.

"That was..." I start, though I don't have an appropriate adjective currently at my disposal. "That was really..."

"Shhh," she says. Her hand fumbles around for my lips, but ends up resting across my throat. "There isn't anything you could possibly say right now that I would want to hear."

She doesn't say it mean, although it does hurt my feelings. Fortunately, my body has reached the outer limits of wakefulness and I'm asleep before I can think of anything to say that might prove her right or wrong.

The next time I open my eyes it's because a blade of daylight is slipping through a gap in the curtains and shining right in my face.

The Last Good Halloween

I feel around the mattress for Izzy. My hand comes up empty, and I'm stricken with a stomach-tightening desperation, as if something important is about to be lost, or already has been.

It takes me a few minutes of digging around in the sheets and blankets before I find my dispersed clothing. After climbing down from the loft and checking on the still-sleeping Julian, I leave the camper.

The snow has built up over the course of the night. It now sits about eight inches deep, gleaming white under a cloudless sky. It's warming up, and Izzy's boot prints have turned into translucent puddles. I follow them around the side of the Adler's house. Out front, the Roadrunner is covered in snow and looks like something that's hibernating for the winter. I lose Izzy's tracks when they reach the road, so I wander through town for a few minutes until I spot her dark figure standing in the distance, facing the morning sun. She's got a half-smoked cigarette dangling from her fingers.

I come up beside her and stand there, scanning the town of Simms, Montana.

"We should talk about last night," she says without looking at me, "but I don't know what to tell you."

If someone ever wanted to come up with a sex-ed curriculum that would be both useful and keep students' attention, they could start by teaching you what you're supposed to say in this precise situation. Because I don't have a clue.

"Nothing is probably better than the wrong thing," I say.

Izzy nods and closes her eyes dreamily. She takes a puff from her cigarette, then flicks the ash into the snow at her feet.

We seem to be standing on a main street, which has a gas station, a senior citizens' center, and a bar called The Snag. At the far end of the street stands a red brick schoolhouse – easily the largest structure in town. A pickup truck drives past us and, for no reason I can discern, the driver waves to me. I wave back.

Cromley

The desperation I'd felt upon waking suddenly grips me again. "Why did you say you weren't going to be around forever?"

"I did?" she asks, eyes still closed.

"Last night. Right before."

"I can't remember."

I hear a snowmobile revving its tiny jackrabbit engine in the distance. Something has changed between us. I can't tell exactly how, but I'm certain it's not good.

"Let's live here," I blurt.

"That's at least an original reaction after your first time," she says.

"I'll find a job. At that gas station. Or I could be a janitor at that school. You can tend bar at The Snag. This will be great." As I'm talking, something weird happens. It started out as patently absurd, yet now that I've begun to sketch it in, the scenario suddenly seems plausible.

"Maybe the Adlers will let us stay in their camper 'til we get our feet on the ground. Down the road we'll get our own house. Not a mansion, but something. We'll have our own place. Here in Simms. Here in the world."

"We can't do that, Kirby. Be real."

"I *am* being real," I say. And I mean it. This vision I'm having is so real I can almost feel it, and something tells me if I could just get her to see it, to believe it, it'll be true. "There's nothing stopping us," I say. "You know that. You have to."

"You're fifteen."

"I'll lie to people."

"It won't work, Kirby."

"You don't know that, Izzy."

Her eyes regard me tiredly for a moment. I can tell by the sad tilt of her head that she cannot or will not see the life I've laid out for us, thereby dooming it to a short existence in my imagination.

The Last Good Halloween

"We better check on Julian," she says. "If he wakes up and doesn't see us..." She shakes her head.

"Yes," I say, turning. "We better."

She drops her cigarette and it disappears into the snow with a fast-dying sizzle.

Chapter 18

His and hers matching jack-o-lanterns grin at us from the Adlers' porch while we scrape off the Roadrunner. As the snow goes, so does our dusty camouflage. I'm not sure how effective it's been, but from here on out we'll be exposed.

While the engine warms up, Felix and Mary try one last time to convince us to stay for breakfast. Even out in front of their house I can smell the bacon grease and pancakes, and I have a hunch Felix will call them flapjacks, which is a word I love and would love to hear him use. But there's nothing they can say or do to stall us any longer. I'm ready to put Simms behind me. It's as if I wouldn't mind spending either the rest of my life here or not one second more.

The Adlers actually seem sad to see us go. We drive off and they stand there on the porch, flanked by their carved pumpkins, waving until we're out of sight and probably even longer.

A few minutes outside Simms, we come upon a bison-shaped snowplow. We tuck in behind it and follow its lead. We're not breaking any speed records, but compared to the terrifying whiteout miles I logged last night, it's a relief. As my eyes settle on the strip of black asphalt the plow is unpeeling before us, my mind is free to ponder the foreign and frightening landscape that lies between me and the mute figure in the backseat.

The Last Good Halloween

She's given up on the beret, so her hair is a choppy mess of black tangles. She must have washed off her makeup in the Adlers' bathroom last night; she's got dark circles under her eyes and her cheeks seem hollow. It's not like she's any less beautiful to me – she just looks like something fragile that's been left out in bad weather for too long. She's staring through the side window, seemingly absorbed by the iceberg-colored mountains floating silently past. There's a calmness to her I've never seen before. She's found some quiet center inside herself and chosen to set up mental shop there.

I think I'm starting to understand that maturity might simply be the ability to force yourself to *not* do something you desperately, achingly *want* to do. And that's it. In which case, I hope Izzy's silence here is masking the fact that she's doggedly fighting the same internal fight I am. Because right now, every fiber of my being is telling me to pull this car over, grab her by the shoulders and tell her in no uncertain terms that I want to be with her and no one else. Each second I sit here at the wheel driving, pretending that's not how I feel, is another reluctant step towards maturity.

Which I can now say definitively sucks. In fact, it's causing actual, physical pain in the back of my throat, like I accidentally swallowed a big pill sideways.

"I feel so much better than I did last night," Julian says, stretching his arms over his head. "I hope I didn't miss much."

"Nothing special," I say. A glance in the rearview mirror catches Izzy looking at me then looking away. "The Adlers were nice people."

"Up until I saw them this morning," he says, "I thought they were part of a dream I was having."

"We were worried," Izzy says. "We kind of lost you after that phone call with your parents."

Julian bites his lips and tucks his hands under his thighs. "Did I ever tell you, my dad promised me I could have this car?"

"*This* car?" I ask.

"All I have to do is get straight A's both semesters this year."

"That's fucked up."

"Why?"

"It's cruel," I say. "He might as well tell you it's yours if you can fit a thousand pieces of bubblegum in your mouth. It's not going to happen."

I know what I'm saying is mean and unnecessary. I know it as soon as the words are out of my mouth, but saying them is helping to ease the pain in my throat.

"It's a tease, Julian, to make you work harder. He knows he'll never have to make good on it."

"Talk about cruel," Izzy says.

"You never know," he says. "I get pretty decent grades."

"Listen," I say, "Newsflash: Your parents are getting divorced!"

Julian looks at me a moment, mouth frozen somewhere between a smile and a grimace.

"Buddy, you better open your eyes. Once they split, you can forget about this car or anything else because everything goes up for grabs."

Based on the way I just defined maturity, I'm not ranking very high, and yet I don't care. Some evil sector of my brain is deriving pleasure from this. Maybe even sustenance.

"You don't have to be such a dick," Izzy says.

"Am I lying? Am I telling him something that's *not* true?"

"Ignore him, Julian. You don't have to listen to him."

"It's okay," Julian says, his composure oddly intact. "Being friends with Kirby I've come to expect these bumps every once in a while. You hang around him long enough you practically learn to predict them."

How is this happening? How is he saying these things? This is not the Julian I know.

The Last Good Halloween

He goes on, "Things haven't worked out the way he wanted so far on this trip. I can't really blame him for taking a few swings at me."

I don't know how he's done it. He's managed to both insult and disarm me. It's like being made fun of by Gandhi. All I can do is sputter, "Things worked out for me pretty well back in Simms!"

Izzy flashes me a betrayed look in the mirror.

"What?" I ask her reflection. "What?"

"Maybe we should all just be quiet 'til we get to Missoula," Julian says.

And the conversation is effectively over.

In the prickly silence that ensues, I'm able to do a post-mortem on what just took place. It seems to me we're all guilty (though me especially) of saying the truth. Which makes it hard to assign much blame. Still, we're on our way to Missoula and to what will likely be a monumental, if not watershed, moment in my young life, and it'd be nice to do that with two people who don't hate my guts.

An hour after anyone last spoke, remorse properly dialed up, I say, "I can't change who I am."

No one says anything to this, so I add, "I shouldn't have said what I did."

Again, no one says anything, though the silence that follows feels a little less prickly.

The roads on the western side of the pass show no signs of the snow that socked us in last night. In fact, the closer we get to Missoula, the better the weather turns. Fragrant pine forests run the entire spectrum of greens, and sunlight twinkles off the surface of a river that plays a game of leapfrog with the road. The scene is so goddamned beautiful I half expect to see chicks in bikinis inner-tubing, or bears playing poker around a felt table, or some other beer commercial sight gag.

Cromley

By the time we exit the highway and roll through downtown Missoula, it's warm and sunny and people are strolling around in shorts and T-shirts. They're biking and jogging and walking dogs like it's the middle of August and not late October.

The first couple people Izzy asks for directions shrug their shoulders, until a guy wearing a dusty poncho tells us what we're looking for is only a few blocks away. The Uptown Motel is on a quiet side street, sandwiched between two busy thoroughfares. It's a small, dumpy-looking place made out of dull brick. It's got a tall sign out front with "Uptown" written in a white strip of cursive neon, and "Motel" in a blockier yellow. Three homeless-looking men are standing on the sidewalk out front. It's hard to tell if they're motel guests or just unaffiliated loiterers, though their long hair and ratty clothes give the establishment a thoroughly seedy aspect either way.

We parallel park across the street, in front of the county courthouse, which is a large gray-stone structure. It has a regal, been-there-forever look to it, a marked contrast to the Uptown, which seems both squalid and ephemeral. Among the dozen or so cars in the motel lot is a familiar Saab 900.

"That's his car," I say.

I can only tell it's his by double-checking the license plate, because the car itself looks so different. There's a circular dent in the rear quarter panel, as if someone had head-butted it. The antenna is bent at an acute angle. And the windshield is heavily bug-splotched.

"I wonder what room he's in," Julian says.

I shake my head.

"We could do a stakeout," Izzy suggests.

"What if he doesn't come out for a long time?" I say, because now that we've actually tracked him down I'm kind of scared to see him.

"Let me try something." Before I can ask Julian what he intends to try, he's shouldered open his door and is striding across the street.

The Last Good Halloween

"What's he doing?" I ask Izzy.

She shakes her head. "You have to admire his enthusiasm."

Julian pulls open the glass door to the office. There are no windows from our angle, so we lose visual contact once he goes in. He's on his own. Nothing we can do but wait.

There's a lot of record-straightening I'd like to set with Izzy, now that we're alone, but my thoughts have jumped to the Bradley-track, and if I try to switch back to the Izzy-and-me-track right now, I'd probably just make things worse. So I sit there, eyes watching the office door, fingers doing a drumroll loop on the steering wheel, and the silence ballooning from uncomfortable to unbearable.

The office door swings open. Julian's got a bouncy stride as he crosses the street.

"What happened?" Izzy asks when he gets back to the car.

Julian is breathless with excitement. "I was going to do this thing I saw in a movie where you ask to leave a note for someone and then you watch which cubbyhole they put the note in. But when I got there they didn't have any cubbyholes."

"What did you do?" Izzy asks.

"I asked them which room Bradley Kellogg was staying in, and they told me 213."

My eyes have already found the room. It's at the south end of the building, overlooking the tiny parking lot. There's a window next to the door, but the curtains are pulled tight.

"You want to knock?" Izzy asks me.

"Let's scope it out a few more minutes. See what happens."

I unroll the window and force myself to keep breathing.

The three derelicts in front of the motel have a paper bag-wrapped bottle that they're passing among themselves. One of them lays down on the sidewalk and the other two start laughing so hard they have to hold themselves up against the wall. After a few minutes, I realize the one lying down is a woman. I have no idea what her relationship to the two men is. Eventually, their bottle runs empty and one of the guys smashes it against the curb. If the three of them were more sober, they'd probably notice how suspicious the three of us look, sitting in our car looking at them.

A flutter of movement on the second floor. The door to 213 opens. A figure partially emerges. He stands there a moment, looking inside, as if he were having a conversation with someone in the gloomy interior. Then he steps out onto the walkway and closes the door. He rests his hands on the railing and takes in a deep, satisfied breath as he surveys the city before him.

"Ummm," Julian says, "that's not your stepdad."

It's not. But he *is* familiar. Scraggly blond hair that's long in the back. He's even wearing the same puffy vest he had on the last time I saw him in front of my house. A queasy feeling washes over me. This was a mistake – all of it.

"Are you sure they said Room 213?" Izzy asks.

The guy goes down the staircase. He hops into a car and when it backs out from behind a pickup, I can see it's the same Chevy Lumina he was in before.

"What would you guys think if I said let's just forget this whole thing?" I ask.

Izzy and Julian exchange a look, each of them silently pleading for the other to answer.

"I don't know if that's what you really want," Izzy says tenderly.

"How would you know what I want?"

"Kirby, as long as you've come all this way, you ought to see it through."

"Do you want me to knock on the door?" Julian offers. "I can make something up. I doubt he'll recognize me."

"If anyone's going to knock it should be me," I say. "Give me a second to get my head together."

Before I can even start to do that, though, the door swings open again. This time the figure that emerges is Bradley. He's wearing a blue tracksuit and cat-eye sunglasses. Slung over his shoulder he's carrying a duffle bag that matches his tracksuit. Neither the clothes, the sunglasses, nor the duffle bag are things I've ever seen before. They are new, purchased sometime between his departure from our house and now.

"That's him."

"The mythical Bradley," Izzy says. "It's like seeing Bigfoot."

He does a stretchy thing on the stairs before descending and striding purposefully toward his Saab.

"Aren't you going to talk to him?" Julian asks.

My hand is on the door handle, but my legs are stiff, non-compliant.

"I need more observational data," I say, though the truth is all the observational data I've collected thus far is telling me to abort this mission, turn around and go back to Billings and never speak of any of it again.

The Saab starts with a smoky burp, which could be a harbinger of trouble on the horizon if he doesn't find a mechanic he trusts to look at it.

By the time he backs out, I've got the Roadrunner ready to pursue. It turns out, though, Bradley ends up going south, while we're facing north, so I have to wait for a gap in the traffic to do a U-turn.

By that time, his car is far enough gone that we've lost sight of it. We cross over a bridge and into a residential section. All of us are staring at the road ahead and peering as far down the side streets as we can.

"There it is!" Julian shouts. "Over there."

It's a little strip-mall whose predominant tenant is a place called Bullet Gym. The Saab is parked out front. Bradley's inside by the time we pull up.

"What do you want to do?" Izzy asks.

"I'm not going to hassle the guy while he's working out."

Cromley

"We can't keep following him around forever," she says. "At some point you have to talk to him."

"I know," I say. "I know. As soon as he comes out. I promise."

There's a college sports game going on today – probably football, though I'm not positive. The stadium must be nearby because the sidewalks are snarled with people wearing rust-and-silver jockwear. Others are wearing Halloween costumes. There's a mummy, two guys done up like skeletons, three girls dressed as zombie cheerleaders. Some of the fans have horns they're blasting; some are shouting chants. Most of them are carrying plastic cups of beer. It becomes so crowded I have to get out of the car and stand under a nearby tree in order to keep the gym door in sight. Which isn't all bad because it's nice to be on my own for a bit, away from Julian and Izzy. Gives me a chance to think.

It must be forty minutes before Bradley finally emerges from the gym. His hair is shower-slicked and his cheeks have a healthy post-exercise glow. Just as he turns for his Saab, just as I begin to concoct an excuse for not approaching him, he freezes, one foot caught mid-stride.

Slowly, he pivots back toward me. He stands there, staring. He takes his sunglasses off. This is the man who, until recently, was the closest thing I've ever had to a father. This is the man who bore witness to significant chunks of my childhood. There's nothing for me to do but wave. Which is what I do, giving him a single, slow flipper-sweep of the right hand.

He looks around to see if he recognizes anyone with me. When he's sure I'm alone, he approaches cautiously. I cross the stream of sports revelers on the sidewalk so I can meet him halfway, in the middle of the Bullet Gym parking lot.

Bradley and I were never huggers before he left, and I'm pleased to see that neither of us feels compelled to change that dynamic, despite these powerfully different circumstances. We perform a crisp three-pump business shake – it's the most natural thing we could do in this moment.

Up close, I can see how different he looks. Though he was never heavy, his face is leaner, and the cleft in his chin more pronounced. He's also let his hair grow out – not what you'd call long or anything, just enough to creep over the ears. But most shocking, most clearly out of character, and most obviously indicative that something has changed, is the fact that he now has a tiny, barely-noticeable earring in his right ear. The old Bradley never would have done something that's so obviously a reach outside the confines of his demographic; in fact, I'm pretty sure the old Bradley used to make fun of men who wore earrings. The sight of that little silver post glinting from his earlobe is enough to make me hold onto his already-shaken hand long enough so that he has to forcibly remove it from my grasp.

"You're looking well," I tell him, because I think this is a thing adults say when they don't know what they're supposed to say.

Somewhere in the near distance a marching band kicks up – sour brass, flighty woodwinds, bass drums resonating in my chest.

"You're looking well, too," he says.

"I spent last night in a camper. And I've basically subsisted on beef jerky for the last day and a half, so I know I can't possibly look well, Bradley."

"Fair enough," he says, smiling in that way people do when someone they know says exactly what they expected.

"So, an earring," I say. "That's a bit of a stretch, don't you think?"

"What are you doing here? How did you get here?"

I glance back at the Roadrunner. Izzy and Julian are pressed against the window glass. When she sees me look over, Izzy does a thumbs-up, though it's tentative, like it might be more of a question than a suggestion.

"It's too long to get into," I say, turning back to Bradley.

"Does your mother know you're here?"

Cromley

"I don't think knowing where I am right now would make Debbie feel a whole lot better, do you?"

Bradley readjusts the duffle bag on his shoulder. He looks up at the people heading toward the stadium.

"I read that letter you sent Debbie. That's how we figured out you were staying at the Uptown Motel. Then we followed you here."

A look of panic seizes his face. I'm not sure what part of what I just said caused this to happen.

"When I say *we*, I mean me and my two friends who're helping me. Debbie's not here, in case you're worried about that."

"So you know," he says, his voice tight, eyes shifting everywhere except on me.

"Know what?"

His face loosens and he smiles in that same way he did a few seconds ago. He puts a hand on my shoulder. "Let's take a stroll, Kirby."

We venture out onto the sidewalk and enter the slipstream of migratory fans. Bradley is quiet for a few minutes. Before he can develop his own strategy for this conversation, I decide to strike preemptively with one of the deadlier weapons in my arsenal.

"Harley Doherty, that guy from across the street, has moved in. He and Debbie are shacking up and it might be getting kind of serious."

Bradley nods for a moment. "I'm not surprised," he says. "I think there might've been something going on there for a while."

No trembling hands. No dilating pupils. No green skin. No tearing his clothes off and setting out to hulk-smash this familial interloper.

"Wait a minute." I turn to face him, but he keeps walking, so I have no choice but to follow. "I can't believe you're not going back to Billings right now to claim what's rightfully yours."

"You can't own someone," he says.

The Last Good Halloween

"Aren't you mad about what I just told you? Don't you feel the slightest bit jealous or possessive? You must. I saw what you wrote. You said you still loved Debbie. You haven't given up – I know it. Harley means nothing to her. You can get rid of him without breaking a sweat. I'll even help."

"One thing I've figured out recently, Kirby, is you can't make someone do something they don't want to."

"Actually, Bradley, I think history's taught us over and over that that's *exactly* what people can and do do."

"Not when it comes to this sort of thing."

"What the hell is going on with this defeatist attitude? How can you turn your back on the last six years like they never happened?"

"Things are more complicated than you realize," he says, his voice drifting.

All at once I realize that when he said you can't make a person do something they don't want, he wasn't talking about Debbie. He was talking about himself.

"But you said in your letter a divorce wasn't the answer," I tell him, as if this were a promise he'd made to me. "It meant you'd failed."

"That's how I felt at the time," he says, shaking his head slowly. "Since then, certain things have crystallized."

The marching band drumbeat shifts up-tempo and the horn section begins tooting "The Eye of the Tiger." A pickup truck whose bed is crammed full of past-their-prime jocks wearing their old football uniforms cruises past, its horn bleating in time to nothing. I really, really, really wish we weren't having this conversation right here.

The pace on the sidewalk has slowed. The fans are getting backed up, restless. I can smell charcoal grills cooking meat and I feel desperately hungry – hungry in a way that even if I were to eat forever I might not feel full. I've mishandled this encounter. But maybe with a different approach I can salvage things. Maybe there's still hope.

"I'm sorry, okay?" I grab Bradley's wrist and squeeze it. "I'm sorry for the time I made you clean that fish. I'm sorry for the time I quit doing magic. I'm sorry for whatever happened with the Doug Henning show tickets. I'm sorry for being mean to your sister – back when we visited her, and again yesterday. I'm basically sorry for every possible thing I ever did that might have made your life less than perfect. I'm sorry and I can be better and I will be."

Bradley's looking at me now. His eyes seem so sad. I've finally gotten to him. "I'm sorry too," he says.

"Great," I say. "Clean slate. Now we can start over and make sure we get it right this time."

"Kirby," he says, his eyes looking directly into mine, "I'm gay."

Physically, I hear his words. They enter my ear canals and reverberate against my eardrums and those vibrations go through whatever process it is that translates them into language. But it no longer feels like it's my body that's doing any of this. I'm seeing myself from the outside, from a distant and filtered perspective:

Young Kirby, embarrassed by what he's just heard, looks around quickly to see if any of the people nearby are listening. When he's convinced that Bradley's words remain privy to only the two of them, he looks back at his stepfather, hoping to detect a smirk or an impish grin, quickly followed by assurances that this was all a joke. He's greeted only by Bradley's serious countenance. Kirby is unsure what to feel, what emotion makes the most sense. It's the first time he's heard anyone openly admit such a thing and his first thought is, Does that – through some transitive property – make *me* gay? But he remembers last night with Izzy and realizes the absurdity of the question. And while he may feel some relief in that knowledge, he can't deny the feeling that what he's just heard will stay with him for a very long time. Then he notices his stepfather's mouth is moving again, and, quite suddenly, he's back inside his own body.

"Kirby, can you hear me?" Bradley asks. "Are you okay?"

"Sure," I say. "Sorry, I'm just trying to figure out what this means."

"Hey, if you do, let me know." He smiles, but then stops smiling when he sees I'm not amused.

The crowd surges forward again and we are propelled with it. Someone nearby is blowing a referee's whistle over and over and over.

"Does Debbie know about this?"

He nods. "It's not something you really have control of. Believe me."

I'm playing in a league of adulthood here that lies way beyond my ken. "So that guy that came out of your hotel room?"

"Uh-huh."

"You know he showed up at our house a while back. He has terrible manners."

"We talked about that," Bradley says. "Mark and I were having some difficulties at the time. I didn't mean for him to involve you."

In the distance, I can hear someone making announcements over a loudspeaker. The words are lost in an echo-y haze.

"What would Ronald Reagan say about all of this?" I blurt because it's the only thing I can think of at this point.

Bradley looks off, thoughtfully contemplating the Great Communicator. "I'd like to think in his heart he'd take a libertarian view of it," he says. "Though I have a feeling those Moral Majority types really got their hooks into him."

The stadium finally swings into view, a gray metallo-concrete structure that rises up above the surrounding houses.

"Are you sure it wasn't Debbie or me that pushed you away?"

"I wish," he says, and it sounds like he really means it. "It'd be nice to have someone else to blame. You have no idea how much I've beaten myself up over this."

Cromley

"I have to be honest," I say. "When I set off to find you, and all the time planning it, this was never something I expected."

"What did you expect?"

"Lots of things, but not this. It's highly..."

"Inconclusive?" he offers. Bradley's always been a word-offerer. Yet up until this moment, I'd forgotten that particular habit. I wonder how many other traits of his I've already forgotten and how many more I'll forget in the coming months. It's as if I can see him being erased right before my eyes.

"Not really inconclusive," I say. "I mean, this clearly marks the conclusion of something. It's not like I can do much to persuade you to come home, so it's definitely a conclusion. I guess I don't know what word I need."

He smiles for a moment and then stops smiling. Our time is very near its end.

"Should I be mad at you or something?" I ask.

"Maybe," he says. "That'll probably come later."

Bradley and I have followed the crowd right up to the stadium entrance. We're next in line for a game neither of us has tickets for.

"Come on," Bradley says. "Let's get out of here."

He puts his hand on my shoulder to steer me as we turn and thread our way back through the crowd, back the way we came, two salmon swimming against the stream.

Chapter 19

Somewhere behind us I can hear thousands of voices come together in a single sustained *Ohhhhhhhh* that slowly crescendos until, on some unseen cue, it bursts and fragments back into thousands of separate voices again. The game must have just started. The future, for those people, has arrived. As for me, I'm not quite ready. There's still something missing from this encounter, some piece that needs to be put into place before I'll be okay with going home.

"Hey, Bradley, can we stop for a second?"

He nods. "Sure."

There's a half-assed little park across the street – tiny, but at least it's got a bench, which seems like as good a place as any to sort out the last of my unresolved feelings. We sit down next to each other, both of us facing straight ahead as if we were strangers who'd just happened to need a rest at the same time.

"All those years you were with Debbie and me, did you, like, know you were gay or something?"

"Kind of, but kind of not."

"So you were faking it?"

"Not very well, I'm afraid."

"Are you really sure about this? I mean, is there any chance you're not?"

The Last Good Halloween

He smiles at the corners of his mouth.

"After all, you've changed your mind once. It's possible it could happen again, right?"

Bradley shakes his head slowly. "That's not really how it works."

I can hear the bass line of the marching band in the distance, though I can't pick out the melody anymore.

"You know, Kirby, out of all the people I've told, you've probably had the most decent, most genuinely human reaction."

"Is that supposed to make me feel better?"

"I don't know," he says. "This is all foreign to me too."

The wood plank of the park bench feels cold on my butt cheeks.

"I've never met anyone who was gay before." As I say this I realize it's technically not true, since I'd met Bradley a long time ago, I just didn't *know* he was gay.

"It's a big world, Kirby."

"Sometimes I think it's too big."

"It's only going to get smaller," he says. "From here on out."

A thick bank of clouds is moving in from the west. Soon, it'll blot out the sun, and the morning's reprieve from autumn will be finished.

"Is there any last piece of advice you can give me?" I ask, still seeking the thing that will make this trip make sense.

"Look at me," he says. "You saw the dump I'm living in. I'm clearly in no position to be dispensing wisdom."

"Is that the best you can do? Because this is basically it for you and me. This is your last chance to mold a young life."

Bradley seems not to have considered this. He turns to me. His eyes are searching for something, though I'm not sure what.

"I'm lousy at advice," he says, "and trying to give you some would imply I know something you don't, which, at this point, I highly doubt."

Cromley

He scans the perimeter of this mini-park for a few seconds. "I can tell you something that might be useful though," he says.

I nod my head for him to keep going.

"I met your father once."

"What?"

His hands, which had been resting comfortably on his lap, begin fidgeting. "It was a long time ago. You weren't home. Debbie had something of his that he needed and she wanted me to be there when he came to collect it."

"The Original Biological Contributor?"

A dozen questions spring to mind at once, and in that querulous glut, none of them are able to force their way out – like when all three Stooges are trying to get through the same door at the same time.

"I only bring it up to tell you he wasn't the world's most savory character," Bradley says. "Without going into details, I think your mom made the right decision in keeping him from being part of your life. That might sound harsh, but I don't mean it that way."

"I don't see why you're telling me this."

"Flawed as I was, I think I managed to do a better job as your father than he would have."

This is the first thing he's said today that makes me genuinely mad. I want to scream at him: *No fucking shit! I'm better off without Rod or any of the other losers that came after. And I'm way better off WITH you!* But I know there'd be no point. The Bradley-Returns Index is frozen at absolute zero – hell, the BRI, for all intents and purposes, doesn't even exist anymore. Saying those things would only make us both feel worse. So instead, I say, "I guess the grass isn't always greener."

"In this case, that's the truth."

We're both quiet for a few moments. We've reached a conversational impasse. He can't tell me anymore and I can't extract anything else from him. Continuing along these lines will only piss me off even more. Our time together is at an end.

"Shall we?" I say.

"I guess," he says.

We take up beside each other on the sidewalk again. Up ahead I see Izzy standing near the Roadrunner. She's talking with a straggling sports reveler, and I can tell by his arm-vectoring that he's giving her directions to some place north of where we are. A small whirlwind of leaves comes to life on the sidewalk directly in front of us, but we walk right through it.

By the time we've reached the Bullet Gym parking lot, Izzy's gotten whatever directions she'd been seeking and rejoined Julian in the car.

Bradley and I pull up for our final good-bye. The moment seems to require some kind of parting gesture, some tangible exchange to serve as proof that this encounter really took place. In my pocket, I've still got that junior high graduation photo of me, Debbie and Bradley, the one where we look like a real family. But I kind of like that picture and wouldn't mind keeping it. Then something occurs to me and before I can decide if it's a good idea or not, I've got my wallet out and I'm extracting a folded-up dollar bill from behind my learner's permit.

"What's this?" he asks as I press it into his palm.

"It's the Doug Henning dollar."

His eyes widen for a moment. When he looks at me again, he seems like he might be near tears.

"It feels like you're trying to wound me, Kirby."

"I'm not," I say, though I might be. "I just wanted you to have something to help you remember that it wasn't all bad."

"I won't need this to help me do that." He places the bill back in my hand as if it had just burned him.

"In that case, any message you want me to pass on to Debbie?" I ask as a way to speed this thing up.

Cromley

He shakes his head. "I think it's better if I communicate directly with her."

"Fair enough." I re-stash my bill and put my hand out and hold it there. Bradley doesn't immediately take it.

"Try to be happy, Kirby. Whatever situation you find yourself in, try to be happy."

"Nice," I say. "Really profound." Then I re-cock my hand. I'm no longer in the mood for advice. Anything he could say now would only confuse the situation, make it more sticky than it needs to be.

"Take care, Bradley. And best of luck to you in all your endeavors."

There's a little tic in his face somewhere around his eyes. It tenses and then relaxes. Afterwards he doesn't look the same as before. He takes my hand.

"You too, Kirby."

Just before I turn around, it looks like he wants to say something else, like some other thought had just occurred to him, but I don't wait.

I turn, I walk, I get in the car, I start the ignition, I leave. I don't even look back as I'm pulling away. That's maturity.

"Home again, home again, jiggety-jig," I intone. It's an old jingle Debbie used to say when I was a kid, and, while I've never used it before, I'm desperate for something to ward off the gloom that's pressing in on all sides.

Julian and Izzy say nothing. They've intuited that Bradley's not coming back and they've wisely chosen not to push me on it. Still, I wish I could pry something out of them to inject a little levity.

"Next stop, Billings!" I call out in a train conductor's voice – just vamping for anything to fill the wretched silence.

"Actually," Izzy says, leaning forward into the front seat's airspace, "there's one more stop we need to make." Her face is somber, her voice small. "Take a left at that next light."

The Last Good Halloween

The Missoula bus station is a cinder block building on the north side of the train tracks. The only bit of color on the whole structure is the red and blue Greyhound sign, and even that looks like it's been years since its last cleaning. The place is largely deserted except for a group of grungy hippies crouched near the front door, passing a cigarette around in a circle.

"Why are we stopping here?"

When I glance in the mirror, Izzy responds with a look that says she really doesn't want to spell it out. Fortunately, Julian can't see her look.

"Seriously, what's at the bus station?" he asks.

"Buses," Izzy says. Then when that fails to draw a laugh, she adds, "And me."

"Why?"

"We're not that far from Seattle. I've got some friends there."

"You can't just leave," Julian protests.

"Actually, I kind of can."

"Why would you?"

"I have to get out of Billings, you guys. You have no idea how badly that place is killing me."

"You're not coming home with us?" Julian asks.

"I've got enough cash to get a ticket from here. If I don't do it now, I might never get the chance again."

"What about typing class?" I ask. "You were doing so well in it."

She tilts her head and gives me a puzzled look.

Julian and Izzy hug outside the Roadrunner. And when they do, she really does look more like his mother than a friend. As she peels herself away, I can see his eyes are red and raw.

"Walk with me, Kirby," she says.

We drag our feet to the bus station entrance. A guy in an army uniform is out front now. He's trying to make a call on the payphone, but the person on the other end of the line can't seem to hear him. He's got a finger in one ear and he keeps saying: "Hello, hell—hello, hello, hell— hello..."

"I guess this is what you meant last night when you said you wouldn't be around forever."

The sidewalk is dotted with black gum-spots. The aroma of cigarette smoke and bus exhaust is heavy in the air – the unmistakable smell of mass transit.

"It was in the back of my mind for a while. Then once I realized we were coming to Missoula, it kind of hit me." Her dark hair is still tangled. Her face is clean and open, but tired. As I look at her, I can't stop myself from seeing her picture in black and white, posted on the side of a milk carton. Hair badly bleached, too much makeup, a black eye – it's too much to bear.

"Don't do this," I say.

"There's nothing for me back in Billings," she says.

"Except me."

She bites her lip and looks away – at the army guy still trying to be heard on the phone, at the hippies lounging on the dirty concrete.

"I'm glad we did what we did, back in Simms last night," she says. "I'm going to remember that for a long time."

She's looking at me now, her dark eyes waiting for me to agree with her. And while I'm tempted to withhold that validation, keep it back as a way of protesting her running off to Seattle, I know I'll regret that spite for a long time if I do, so I say, "Me too."

She cracks a relieved smile. Behind us, inside the station, some kind of announcement is made over a loudspeaker. The hippies begin to collect themselves.

"Can I ask you one last thing?" I say.

She draws in a shaky breath. She nods, though I can tell she's worried I'll ask something that might send her over an emotional cliff.

"Why did you hang out with me all this time?"

The Last Good Halloween

She shakes her head, not comprehending.

"You spent all this time with me. In case you haven't noticed, I'm a pretty big loser."

Her face brightens. "In case *you* haven't noticed," she says, leaning closer, "losers are some of my favorite people."

She moves in the rest of the way, and we kiss. I was expecting it this time, so I'm able to give as well as I get. It's not a long kiss and it's not super-tonguey or anything. It's a good-bye kiss, begun with the knowledge of how it will end.

And then it ends.

"Here, take this," I say, handing her the bill that Bradley wouldn't accept.

"What is it?"

"It's something that's supposed to mean something."

She unfolds it and reads the inscription. "'Wishing you magical joy'?"

I nod. "Keep it."

"That's kinda corny, isn't it?"

"Yes, it is," I say. "One hundred percent."

Izzy smiles again. She refolds the bill and, for no good reason, she sniffs it before tucking it into her jacket pocket.

Then she steps back toward the glass door. She looks past me to Julian and waves. She steps back again and keeps her hand raised. She holds it there, unmoving, like the old-time movie Indians saying, "How."

She's at the door now. She opens it without turning around. She's inside.

I wait a full sixty seconds to see if there's any more to the story, some last minute change of heart, or just-kidding coda. But there isn't.

Chapter 20

We're on the interstate now, heading east towards Billings. The roads are clear, so we're able to move along at a pretty good clip, though the miles seem to barely melt away. The brown fields surrounding us look like they could go on forever.

Julian and I haven't talked in a while. I think he's stunned that we somehow met the objective of our quest, yet didn't achieve our goal. Life, as far as he understands it, isn't supposed to work that way.

I'm quiet because I'm remembering something from the Bradley Era. Some years ago, the two of us set out on an ambitious undertaking to get through all the *Lord of the Rings* books. Each night, Bradley would read a chapter to me right before bed. It became our thing for a while. And we made it pretty far. But eventually, we stopped about a third of the way through *The Return of the King*. I never did find out how it all ended. This was one case, however, where my failure to finish something was not caused by me simply losing interest in it.

I remember as we read – as Frodo got closer to Mount Doom and further from his home in the Shire – I remember being gripped with worry and, yes, even dread, at how he and Sam would get back when it was all over. Every obstacle they got past meant one more thing standing between them and home. And, while that was troubling, what really caused me to put an end to the project, to summarily walk away, was the fact that I kept thinking about how depressing that trip back was going to be. Their adventures were over, and life – the exact same life as before, only more plain and ordinary because of what they'd done – was the only thing waiting for them.

When people think about going on adventures, they never think about going home, or what's waiting for them when they get there.

"Did he say *why* he wasn't coming back?" Julian's still trying to wrap his mind around what's happened. Though I think his concern here is at least partially proprietary. If he knows the why in *my* scenario, he might be able to divine the reasons why his own family is on the verge of collapse. I haven't gotten into the particulars of my conversation with Bradley though, partly because Julian might not approve due to his Christianness, and also because it's not something Bradley probably wants out there.

"I think he and my mom have just kind of run their course," I say.

He shakes his head. It's not very useful and I'm sorry about that.

"That sucks for you," he says at last.

"For everyone," I say.

A black and white highway patrol car flies past going the opposite direction. I double-check the Roadrunner's speedometer. The needle is steady at fifty-six.

"I'm glad I came, though," I say. "Just to be sure. I think there's some benefit to knowing."

In the rearview mirror, I can see the patrol car's brake lights illuminate. Then the car dips down into the grassy depression as it crosses over to our side.

"To knowing what?" Julian asks.

"To knowing I'd done everything I could. That sense of completion is definitely worth a lot."

The patrol car is on us in seconds. Aware of what will come next, and feeling oddly relieved, I lift my foot off the gas.

"It's a pretty good feeling," I say, "if you can isolate it from all the others."

The blue lights start swirling. Julian sees them and his body tenses. He braces his hands against the dashboard. The Roadrunner eases to a stop on the shoulder. We're somewhere shy of Butte. It's a flat, wide valley – brown field grass, and in the distance a set of weirdly shaped sandstone outcroppings that look like primitive statues erected for an unresponsive god.

"Thanks for coming with me," I say.

"You know what I don't get," he says, his voice high and tight, "is what it all means."

"What does what mean?"

"This trip. It's like we did it – we actually did it. But I still don't know where that leaves us."

I can see someone moving behind the steering wheel of the patrol car, though no one gets out.

"I don't know," I say. "Life isn't like in the Bible where the things have some hidden message you're supposed to learn. This was just some stuff that happened."

"I don't want it to be over," he says.

"Me neither," I say.

The guy in the patrol car is still moving, maybe talking on the radio. But his door isn't even open yet.

"What's he waiting for back there?"

"Whoa! Look at that!" Julian shouts, pointing to the field just ahead of us.

One single deer is grazing nearby on the scraggly prairie grass. Its coat is gray and dusty, and it blends in so well with the terrain it's barely visible even at fifteen yards away.

The Last Good Halloween

"Look at him. Holy crap." Julian has a sense of wonder in his voice that seems disproportionate to what he's telling me to look at.

The deer is alone and it's medium-sized, not full grown, though definitely not a fawn. I can't even tell if it's a female or male because I know some parts of the year the males don't have antlers. It's just a plain, ordinary, run-of-the-mill mule deer – millions of them everywhere.

"What's taking that cop so long?" I ask. Something about the waiting is making me antsy. There's a burning sensation in my chest and I kind of have to pee.

The deer is hungry, eating ravenously. He seems unaware of the fact that he's standing very near a highway, with cars whipping along at serious, bone-crushing, tendon-tearing speeds.

"Christ," Julian says, "that thing better look out."

I pry my hands off the steering wheel and see that they're shaking. I use one of them to steady the other as I shut the engine off.

"Someone better do something!" Julian shouts.

The deer is now on the gravel strip that runs along the shoulder and he's still drifting toward the pavement. Can he really be that oblivious to the danger around him? It doesn't seem possible.

"Jesus, I can't look," Julian shouts. "Someone should do something!"

The deer's ribs are visible along its flanks. I can see his yellowed teeth nibbling at the dried-up grass. My eyelids feel tight and twitchy. My mouth has gone dry, and I don't know if I can talk anymore.

"Somebody do something!"

The door to the patrol car finally swings open. A trooper steps out and hitches his pants up by the belt-loops. Then, as if some internal spring has finally been wound past its breaking point, I flip open my door, uncoil my body from the seat, and begin charging at the deer. I read somewhere that in order to haze an animal properly, you need to make yourself seem bigger than you are and make a lot of noise.

"Hey, idiot! You have to pay attention to where you're going!" I'm waving my arms frantically over my head as if I were drowning. "Will you please watch where you're going? For your own goddamn good! No one else is going to watch out for you!"

The deer looks up. His giant deer eyes are wide and frightened and looking past me. Then he turns and, with the clatter of hooves on gravel, takes off in a stiff-legged retreat through the field, heading for the distant hills. If he's lucky, he's got some family back there who's looking for him, waiting, worried sick.

Then I slowly turn around and look at Julian. His small face is peering out the windshield at me and even though it's kind of far, I can see he's smiling, beaming, as wide as I've ever seen. Years from now, decades even, when he tells his friends and future family about this spree we've gone on, I think the thing he might focus on most of all will be what just happened by the side of this road. It will be the thing in his mind that gets the most ink.

As this idea sinks in, I become aware of the rest of my surroundings. A semi-truck rumbles past, its air-horn blaring so loudly it rattles my teeth. Then a voice:

"Freeze! Now! Hands up!"

Behind the Roadrunner, the highway patrolman has taken a position on one knee, gun drawn and held in both hands, pointed at me.

"Now! Get down! Freeze!"

He seems incapable of speaking in complete sentences, which is something I'd like to point out to him except that he's young and appears highly agitated. I think he's overdoing it with the gun, but, hey, what do I know? I'm not about to argue. I draw the line at antagonizing someone when he's got a loaded gun pointed at me. I mean, you have to have limits.

The Last Good Halloween

So I raise my hands high over my head and shout, "Okay, you got me!"

But he doesn't lower his revolver; he keeps it trained on me and I can see him gripping and re-gripping the handle. I can feel the cool air whistling through my armpits and it gives me a quick chill.

"What do you want from me?" I call out. Then, in case he can't hear me, I get down on my knees. "I give up."

He still doesn't move. So I lay face down on the rough gravel beside the road, lacing my hands behind my head. The ground is cold, ready for the winter snows that'll soon start to fall. I can feel it leeching the warmth out of me. And the thought occurs to me that if I lay here long enough, my body will eventually reach the same temperature as everything else. It'll be as cold as those distant sandstone obelisks.

I can't see the trooper anymore and I can't hear him anymore either. I have no idea what he's doing. So I call out, just to make it clear, "I surrender, I surrender. I give up. I surrender."

Chapter 21

Here's a little advice to all you future or aspiring miscreants: If you're going to commit a law-breaking escapade, try to go home with bodily harm. It might help you get past that initial phase when the parental anger is most volatile, when they're most likely to make snap judgments about your future. They can't send you to reform school if you're laid up in a hospital, fighting for your life with tubes coming out of your wrists and mouth. It would be unseemly. Alas, I came away from the whole thing scrape-free.

I've never seen Debbie more pissed off than the moment she picked me up at the police station in Butte – eyes red, hair a mess, lips as pale as the rest of her face. She silently simmered like the Earth's molten core the entire drive back to Billings. In the nine days since I've been home, she's barely said a word to me. The only real conversation we've had started off with the thesis that a fundamental trust had been broken and concluded with her making good on the threat to send me to the Haverford Military Institute. She's already sent the forms in and everything. Not that I gave her much choice. That little spree I went on was enough to earn me strikes three through thirty-three. We leave for Bismarck the day after tomorrow.

The Last Good Halloween

The only reason I haven't been shipped off yet is because Dr. Byrne wanted to do a series of evaluations to make sure I'm what he calls "stable." On the plus side, they determined that what happened by the side of the highway was not a suicide attempt. So no Velcro shoes for me this time. Other than doctor's visits I've been on supermax home lockdown. Which means that I happened to be here the day Izzy called. She didn't talk much really, just said she wanted to see if I'd gotten home all right. When I told her what had happened, she didn't seem surprised.

"I guess that's one way to end it," she said. I could hear discordant music in the background, but I was too scared to ask her where it was coming from.

"Out in a blaze of glory," I said.

For a moment, the only sound came from the guitars on her end of the line.

"How's the Emerald City treating you?" I asked, trying to make the conversation last, maybe turn it into something meaningful.

"The what?"

"Seattle's nickname. The Emerald City."

"Oh," she said. Her voice sounded far away. "It's okay I guess. Better than Billings."

"This new school they're sending me to is military-based, but it's not like an official U.S. military academy."

"That sounds awful."

"I guess you'd call it a paramilitary academy."

She chuckled lightly and I felt emboldened.

"You'll have to come visit me," I said. "It's in North Dakota."

The line was quiet for a few seconds. Then, "You're probably not going to hear from me for a while, Kirby."

"A while? How long is that?"

"You know," she said.

"Oh," I said, but I didn't know.

Cromley

It's now four days later and I still don't know. Maybe I never will.

In other news, Julian's parents chose not to press charges against me. And they've moved quickly to remove any trace of my influence on their son. They've got him on a steady drip of bible classes and something called "fellowship meetings." But I think he'll be all right. Once they get serious about their divorce, they won't be able to sustain such a rigorous de-programming regimen. I'm confident that the seeds of corruption have been planted deep in Julian and taken root.

I am scared about my own future, though. Based on the pictures I've seen in the brochure for the Haverford Military Institute, it'll probably be a lot like computer camp, but the population set will skew a lot more predatory. This does not bode well for a prey-species like myself. My strategy, as much as you can call it that, is to stay small, get even smaller, hope to avoid being noticed. I'm not optimistic.

Of course, I can't stop thinking about Izzy. Knowing she's out there in the world without me leaves me alternating between feelings of fear and hopefulness. Fear, obviously, because there are a million calamities that could befall her and, frankly, the odds aren't in her favor. Yet I also find myself feeling hopeful at the oddest moments, like any day I might get an anonymous postcard in the mail with a cryptic message that only I'll be able to understand, and maybe it'll give me directions on where to meet her and when. I know this'll probably never happen, but the fact that it *might* happen will have to be enough for now. She never told me how long "a while" would be.

For the past week, Uncle Harley's been taking me to and from my appointments with Dr. Byrne. The first time he and I were alone in the car, he looked at me with what I think was grudging respect.

The Last Good Halloween

"That was a gutsy thing you did," he said as he pulled out of our driveway.

"It's pretty easy for you to be magnanimous when you know I'll be gone in a week."

He sighed and readjusted his grip on the steering wheel. "You definitely climbed a mountain, Kirby. I'm just not sure it was the right mountain."

I didn't respond and he let it go at that, but he kept coming back to it on subsequent visits to the doctor.

"I don't think I'd have enough balls to pull something like that off," he said a couple days later.

"I didn't pull it off, Harley. *Pulling it off* implies that it succeeded. Which it didn't. Because if it did, you'd be gone, and I'd have my old life back."

"Considering how it turned out, was it worth it?" he pressed. "In hindsight?"

"I suppose it had some educational value."

We were waiting at an intersection, red light glaring down on us.

"Such as?"

"I learned that sometimes in order to move on you have to let certain things die."

"That's a tough lesson," he said, frowning. "But a necessary one I guess."

Then, without really thinking about it, I asked him, "What are your intentions here?"

He didn't answer right away, so I took the opportunity to clarify: "With my mother?"

The light turned green and we eased through the intersection. He said, "I think we could have saved ourselves a lot of grief if you'd have asked me that a long time ago."

"Don't bullshit me," I said. "I'm not going to be here much longer and I want to know what your plans are."

Cromley

The question seemed to have genuinely stumped him because for the next minute or so neither of us said a word. Then he pulled over to the side of the road and shut the car off.

"I can't promise anything," he said. "And I suspect a promise wouldn't mean much to you anyway. I can only tell you that I care for your mother and my intentions are pure."

He was looking directly at me, unblinking, I suppose to underscore what he said. I wanted to believe him, but in this Post-Bradley Era, trust is a commodity in rare supply.

So I looked him in the eye, just as hard as he was looking at me, and I told him, "Talk is cheap, Harley."

It's Tuesday night, thirty-six hours before I ship out. Harley and I are sitting in front of the TV. It's dark outside and the warm blue light of the CBS newsroom washes over us.

Debbie's stuck at an opening at the art gallery tonight, so it's just the two of us watching the election returns together. As part of my disillusionment phase with Bradley, I've started to question the whole Reagan phenomenon and, by extension, this Bush character. Mad as I am at Bradley, though, I can't quite bring myself to root for Dukakis.

Harley's drinking a beer, and I'm not supposed to be in here since no-TV is one of my punishments during this pre-Haverford interregnum. Fortunately, we've both agreed to look the other way on each other's improprieties tonight.

Dan Rather appears on the screen to tell us that Bush is "tearing through the South like a tornado through a trailer park." He then goes on to list each state Bush has already taken. Harley is watching the results with the nearly empty bottle dangling from his hand. It's been clear for a while how this election was going to turn out, but I think he was hoping for a miracle, and I can't blame him for that. His hair is wild and his beard is thick, yet underneath it all, I can tell he's fighting back some kind of emotion. Normally, I'd take pleasure in this, but tonight I just can't find the stomach to rub it in.

"Do you want another beer?" I ask.

"Better not." He's peering at the brown bottle in his hand, as if to see what the world looks like through it.

"I suppose you think if Bush wins everything's going to head straight down the toilet."

He looks up at me and squints, though not in an angry way. "It may surprise you to know that I'm an optimist, Kirby. I think things are always getting better."

I try not to chuckle at this but I do. "I don't know if you have the data to back you up on that."

"True," he says, nodding. "But sometimes you have to hold onto things you might not be sure of to help you get through the day."

He drains the last of his beer, then looks at me and musters a smile. Mr. T is sprawled on his back at Harley's feet. Occasionally, one of his paws will dream-flick or he'll let out a mini sleep-yelp as he frolics in the boundless fields of eternal puppyhood.

"Look on the bright side," I say. "I'll be gone pretty soon. You'll have this place to yourself."

"Believe it or not," he says, "I tried to pull some strings for you. I'd rather you stayed here."

"I don't think there are any strings left to pull for me. I'm a man who's run out of strings."

"You cut them yourself, though," he says, not unkindly. "You know that, right?"

We both know it's true. No point even answering.

Around eight o'clock things start to go seriously bad. Ohio gets called for Bush, which the guys on TV say is important because it was part of Dukakis's eighteen state strategy, whatever that is. A little later, the deluge is on. The whole map, it seems, turns red.

Yet Harley hangs tight, keeps watching. He sits there clutching that empty bottle right up through Dukakis's concession and Bush's victory speech. It must be killing him to sit here through all of it, and I'm finding myself impressed by his tolerance for, maybe even resilience to, the humiliation. There's some kind of virtue in that.

After the network is done with its broadcast and they've cut over to the local results, I look up and see a tear in Harley's eye. Nothing over the top, just a small sign of how much this has wounded him. And I find myself strangely moved.

"I didn't cut my strings because of you," I tell him. "It never had much to do with you. Or Debbie for that matter."

"I think I knew that," he says. "But it's good to hear."

"You can tell Debbie too. When I'm gone. Tell her I said that."

He nods and finally sets his bottle down on the floor and forces another smile. He points the remote at the TV, presses the button. The image collapses down into a tiny pinpoint at the center of the screen. We are suddenly surrounded by darkness. And it feels so thick, so impenetrable, that it's hard to know what might be right in front of us. We're safe for the moment, but at some point we'll have to get up from our chairs and stumble out of here, feeling blindly with our hands for a light.

Acknowledgments

A book this long in the making requires the dispersal of more gratitude than this short space can provide, but I'll try anyway. First off, I'd like to thank my family, Brent Sr., Dorothea, Brent Jr., Taya, and Millie, for helping me through various stages of despair and doubt. They've done this so many times it's not even funny.

A gigantic thank you goes to Jerry Brennan, meticulous editor and taker of chances. I hope this book stands as a testament to your vision.

Thanks, also, to the people who have read not only this manuscript but all the others that came before it. Your advice has made me a better writer, even if I wasn't always the best listener: Alex A.G. Shapiro, Dave Cohen, Joe Campana, Pat Bousliman, and Zak Andersen.

Special thanks is merited for Adam Skilken, who taught me that sometimes you just have to go to the river for the afternoon, and for Tony Lipp, who gave me permission to write this story. I'd be remiss if I did not also thank Scott Olsen and Jim Messina, two people who were championing me long before there was much empirical evidence to do so. And big thanks to Ryan Singleton, who has more good ideas than I can keep up with.

I'd also like to thank my writing teachers over the years: Ernest Hebert, Richard Peabody, Bill Lombardi, Kevin Canty, Debra Earling, and Deirdre McNamer. And my colleagues Martha Vertreace-Doody and Terry Clark, who continue to teach me every day. Immense gratitude goes to the Illinois Arts Council, which provided me with not only a much-appreciated funding infusion, but also a much-needed morale boost.

Lastly, I'd like to thank my wife, Natalie Vesga, bringer of light and believer in lost causes. Without you, the world would be a cold dark place indeed.

About the Book

Like most teenagers, Kirby Russo doesn't want much: a calm home life, a couple close friends, a sense of direction and purpose. And a chance to relax with a cocktail now and then. And maybe a quiet bathroom where he can rub one out whenever fantasy and hormones get the better of him. But his world's upended when he comes home from computer camp to find his stepfather gone and his mom sleeping with their neighbor. In short order, he has to plan an epic road trip to save his family. Never mind the fact that he's at that age where you take yourself seriously, but no one else does. Never mind the fact that he doesn't have a car—it's really more like borrowing when it's a friend's parent's car and they won't know it's gone. And never mind the fact that he doesn't know as much about his home life as he thinks he does.

About the Author

Giano Cromley was born in Billings, Montana. His writing has appeared in *The Threepenny Review*, *Literal Latte*, and *The Bygone Bureau*, among others. He is a recipient of an Artists Fellowship from the Illinois Arts Council. He teaches English at Kennedy-King College and lives on Chicago's South Side with his wife and two dogs.

Printed in the USA
CPSIA information can be obtained
at www.ICGtesting.com
JSHW022324140824
68134JS00019B/1283